A BLOODY

Slocum holstered his gun and w

Seated on the ground, .32 in
him with wet eyelashes. On the ground, facedown, was the
body of a man with a pistol in his outstretched hand.

"He came out to kill me."

Slocum nodded, went over and sat down beside her. He
draped an arm over her shoulder. "I know that. This ain't
an easy business."

She holstered the pistol and rose into his arms, burying
her face in his shoulder. "I wanted to celebrate every one of
them being sent to hell—it isn't like that, is it?"

"No, it never is."

She blinked her wet lashes at him. "I still want the rest
of them . . . "

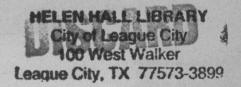

JAKE LOGAN

SLOCUM
AND THE
VENGEFUL WIDOW

DISCARD

J
JOVE BOOKS, NEW YORK

THE BERKLEY PUBLISHING GROUP
Published by the Penguin Group
Penguin Group (USA) Inc.
375 Hudson Street, New York, New York 10014, USA
Penguin Group (Canada), 90 Eglinton Avenue East, Suite 700, Toronto, Ontario M4P 2Y3, Canada
(a division of Pearson Penguin Canada Inc.)
Penguin Books Ltd., 80 Strand, London WC2R 0RL, England
Penguin Group Ireland, 25 St. Stephen's Green, Dublin 2, Ireland (a division of Penguin Books Ltd.)
Penguin Group (Australia), 250 Camberwell Road, Camberwell, Victoria 3124, Australia
(a division of Pearson Australia Group Pty. Ltd.)
Penguin Books India Pvt. Ltd., 11 Community Centre, Panchsheel Park, New Delhi—110 017, India
Penguin Group (NZ), 67 Apollo Drive, Mairangi Bay, Auckland 1310, New Zealand
(a division of Pearson New Zealand Ltd.)
Penguin Books (South Africa) (Pty.) Ltd., 24 Sturdee Avenue, Rosebank, Johannesburg 2196,
South Africa

Penguin Books Ltd., Registered Offices: 80 Strand, London WC2R 0RL, England

This is a work of fiction. Names, characters, places, and incidents either are the product of the author's imagination or are used fictitiously, and any resemblance to actual persons, living or dead, business establishments, events, or locales is entirely coincidental.

SLOCUM AND THE VENGEFUL WIDOW

A Jove Book / published by arrangement with the author

PRINTING HISTORY
Jove edition / March 2007

ISBN: 978-0-515-14264-8

JOVE®
Jove Books are published by The Berkley Publishing Group,
a division of Penguin Group (USA) Inc.
375 Hudson Street, New York, New York 10014.
JOVE is a registered trademark of Penguin Group (USA) Inc.
The "J" design is a trademark belonging to Penguin Group (USA) Inc.

PRINTED IN THE UNITED STATES OF AMERICA

10 9 8 7 6 5 4 3 2 1

Prologue

"You be careful," she said to her excited ten-year-old son, Tobias, as he ran out the back door to join his waiting friends. "And don't get into any trouble today." Her last words fell like water off a duck's back—Tobias was already gone, and she had to put down the mop bucket and reclose the back door that failed to catch. For a moment, she looked across the windswept grass in the too brilliant Kansas sun and watched him with two more boys his age hiking over the grassy rise.

She closed the door and took up the bucket and mop. The store's floor out front waited on her. Her husband, Walter Trent, was busy working on the books at the high desk behind the counter, no doubt looking over some accounts or planning a new order of goods. A short man, Walter stood five-four—two inches shorter than her and fifteen years older. When he sat on the tall stool, his bald head shone in the lamplight as he toiled behind small gold-frame reading glasses that were necessary for him to read figures. A widower a decade before, in his thirties, he'd taken in the frightened, slender, teenage girl from Iowa, orphaned after a war party of red savages killed her family in a raid on their wagon, and he married her so folks wouldn't talk.

"Did Mrs. Carney want red suspenders for her husband or gray ones?" he asked as she plied the mop to the worn pine flooring. "I can't recall."

"Gray. He wouldn't wear red ones."

"That's right, thanks, Wink." Walter always called her Wink. He had such fun with it each time he said it—he always smiled, so she never corrected him and said, "My name is Winkle." His nickname suited her, she decided, wringing out the mop and going for the last stretch. Always good to have this chore finished each morning.

"Don't forget Mrs. Grebby wants blue polka-dot gingham." She carried the half-filled dirty water bucket to the open front door.

"Got it," he said from the rear of the store.

"Morning, Mrs. Trent," Daisy Eaton said, stepping aside for her to exit the store.

"Oh, excuse me, Mrs. Eaton." The straight-backed woman in her forties whom she went past was the wife of the postmaster.

"No problem, my dear. Has Mr. Helm brought the fresh meat yet?"

Wink shook her head; the butcher usually made his deliveries around ten A.M. "Too early, but he'll be along directly."

At the edge of the porch she dashed the water at the hitch rack. Might even settle some dust—before she turned back, she stopped and studied the five riders coming abreast up the dusty ruts called Main Street. There were no other streets.

The big man in the center wore a suit and an expensive high crown hat, and rode with goatskin gloves. On his left, a pimple-faced kid slouched in the saddle, but he looked a lot tougher than most teens—he dressed simple: a cheap brown derby and wash-worn drover's clothing. A thin, hunch-shouldered cowboy rode on the right; he appeared to be too skinny to be healthy. Under a straw sombrero, the fourth rider was a Mexican who sat like a sack of flour in a big-horned saddle that showed off some silver work, and his colorful poncho flapped in the gusts. The fifth rider wore an eagle feather in his black felt hat; it danced and twisted in the wind, slapped the hat—he was Injun, part or maybe a breed. A gold earring in his right ear shone in the sunlight.

Drifters—they came through all the time after making cattle drives and selling them out in Abilene or Hayes. These men were hard cases, but one had to be hard to ever cross all those swollen rivers between the Kansas terminals and the south end of Texas, fight off the rustlers and Indians in the Nation and survive horrific storms and stampedes. She went back inside. Those drovers, like others that had gone past there, would probably stop for a few cigars or candy and ride on. The likes often frequented their establishment passing through, most of them acting anxious to get back to Texas, so they could make the harrowing trip all over again.

The pail and mop on the back porch, she straightened the apron and her blouse then looked over the backside of the small business district of Weyes Corner that consisted of a bank, harness/saddle shop, blacksmith, wagon yard, doc's office, their general store and a few small houses surrounded by a million acres of rolling prairie. On the way through their living quarters, she checked on her curly red-tinted brown hair in the mirror. It looked fine.

She could hear Walter say hello to someone. And give his usual speech about how his business was all cash-and-carry. Must be the drovers she saw riding up.

"I understand cash," the big stranger said, and upon entering the store portion, she recognized the same broad shoulders looking over things like he owned them. Only when his cold gaze fell upon her did she want to shiver. She felt vulnerable under his scrutiny; it forced her to bite her lower lip. His harsh look and small greedy smile was like he saw every inch of her stripped naked as Eve.

"I need a sack of dry beans, a hundred pounds of flour, some lard—"

"I'll get him some lard," she said to Walter, knowing where the green pails were stacked on the far shelf. With a good excuse to exit the man's hard gaze, she held up her dress hem and went for the shortening.

The thin cowboy shouldered a sack of flour and the kid hefted the beans to carry them out. On her toes, she reached for the top pail, and realized Mrs. Eaton was still in the store looking at yard goods and waiting for the butcher's delivery.

"You do understand I said cash-and-carry—" Walter's words coming from over her shoulder shocked her as the weight of the lard pail transferred to her arm. Something was wrong. She twisted to see the two of them separated by the counter—the big man's face exploded, and his gloved hand sprang for the Colt's grips in a side holster swept clear of his coat. A scream of warning in her throat was cut off by closure. The ear-shattering shots slammed Walter against the high desk; then he vanished in the acrid eye-tearing fog of spent black powder.

She dropped to the floor, and the lard can went rolling. Crouched in a ball, she heard Mrs. Eaton screaming at the man, then more shots and a long silence. The nice gray-haired postmaster's wife was dead too. Clenched fists held tight to Wink's face to silence her sobs of self-pity, her quaking body was balled up against the wooden case piled with work shoes. She huddled in wait, and wondered when this killer would walk over to send her to eternity.

Then more shooting began outside, and she heard the gritty footfall of the big man as he ran toward the front door. Something shattered the left plate glass window—Walter would hate that. They costed eighty dollars apiece. More shooting. Why, these madmen must be killing everyone in town.

Then in her trembling fear she recalled the double-barrel shotgun Walter kept loaded under the cash drawer. The thing she hated so and they'd argued over—he had insisted they might need it someday and she'd relented. Wetting her lips, the salty copper taste of blood on her tongue from the lower one she had bitten too hard, she wondered if she could get to the weapon. Crouched, she turned as quietly as possible.

Then, moving in a duckwalk, she reached the back fixture. All she could see was poor Walter's turned-up shoe soles. Her head aching from the pounding blood at her temples, she eased herself closer—no way—no way she'd ever do this—but soon her fingers closed on the smooth wooden stock and she raised the barrel up over the edge and aimed down the flat weld between both humps. The Mexican coming down the aisle looked, wide-eyed, straight into the muzzle, stopped to turn and run, but too late. The hammer cocked, she closed her eyes and squeezed the trigger.

Recoil threw her backward onto the floor, and she hit her head hard on the desk. A barrage of shots riddled cans of peaches and tomatoes on the shelf above her—juices showered down from the punctured tins. Men cursed her. Disregarding everything happening around her, and leaking upon her, she reached over and secured the gun again.

"You get the bank money?" the big man shouted to someone.

On her knees, she moved the wet hair from her face and blinked at the large silhouette in the smoky doorway as she armed the left hammer. For the second time she looked down between both barrels and squeezed the trigger; the stock's butt jammed hard this time against her sore shoulder. Recoil of the second blast still threw her backward onto the floor.

"Damnit, Boss, you're hit!"

"Let's get the hell out of here before she kills all of us."

Her sticky fingers extracted the shells, and she crammed two more fresh ones into the chamber. She could hear them leaving—getting away. She needed to hurry. On her feet, she ran for the front of the store. Tears and peach juice ran down her stained face. Stopped in the doorway, she used the frame to steady herself and the cumbersome gun, then fired again at their fleeing figures. A cloud of black powder smoke veiled her face and burned her eyes, but they were already too far away.

She walked back, absently dropped the scattergun on the

floor and stepped over the bloody, prone body of Mrs. Eaton in her best green dress, whose blank blue eyes stared forever at the tin ceiling squares. Behind the counter she dropped to her knees and gathered Walter's limp head in her lap. With her hand, she carefully straightened the graying fringe around his bald head and rocked him. Rocked him like that might keep him alive or bring him back from the dead.

"Walter, oh, Walter, please don't leave me. What will Tobias and I do without you? I know you wanted him to stay here and work today. See what would have happened to him?" She had to put her finger to her nose to stem the flow. "What will we do without you? Oh, God, why did this have to happen?"

"Where's Doc? What's happened here?"

She gently set Walter aside and raised up on her knees. It was Helm, the butcher. He must have just driven in from his ranch with the meat order. She struggled to her feet and at last used the edge of the counter to pull herself up.

The big, burly man carried the body of a young boy in his arms. Had he been shot in the street too? It was Jimmy Sams—he—he was with Tobias—earlier. Then her gaze met Helms and his sad look couldn't lie to her. He'd brought her even worse news.

With both hands planted on the counter, she tried to swallow. "Did they shoot them too?"

The curly blond-headed boy in his arms, Helm walked the last ten feet to her. "They shot all three of them boys—I guess. Don't know why they shot 'em. I only found 'em— Jimmy's still alive."

"NO!" Her screams were so distant, she could hardly hear them, but she knew from the pain in her throat they were loud enough to be heard for miles.

1

A hot blast of wind swept Slocum's face. He chewed on the toothpick and studied her from the shade of the porch. She sat a powerful blue roan horse and the big-horn Mexican saddle bore some silver work. Even with her dressed in men's clothing, it was hard to hide the fact she was a nice-looking woman in her twenties with a bustline.

"Your name Slocum?" she asked, reining the horse's head up when he coughed.

He nodded. "Been called worse."

"Mine's Wink. I want to hire you."

"Why?"

"Too long of a story to tell out here. Jim Bob Gale sent me. Said you were the man I needed."

Slocum threw away the toothpick and smiled at her. "Where did you find Jim Bob?"

"Abilene—two days ago."

"How did you know I was here?"

"He said you might still be this side of the Nation, if I hurried."

He rubbed his calloused palm over his whisker-bristled mouth and considered her. Nice enough looking woman, 'cept for the edge of anger behind her blue eyes, like impatience might boil out of her any moment. She had something big on her mind if she thought she needed him. He'd better give her a little of his time—besides she wasn't half-bad to look at.

"Get down." He glanced back and considered the faded green batwing doors of the Last Chance. No place for them to talk in there. With a swing of his head, he motioned to the empty benches on the general store's porch down the way and started in that direction.

She hitched the roan at the rack in front of the store and ducked under it. The rail knocked off her cowboy hat and spilled a wealth of reddish-brown curly hair in her face. She straightened and took it up in her hands, to replace the bounty under the hat from her shoulders, where the string on her throat had captured it. Smiling like someone caught in an embarrassing act, she completed the hair fixing, then slid onto the bench a few feet from him.

"Guess you better explain why Jim Bob sent you to me."

"Six weeks ago, five men rode into the crossroads where my husband and I owned a store—Meyer's Corner. Anyway when they left, my husband Walter, the postmaster's wife, the bank teller, a blacksmith and two strangers were lying dead in the street. And then they used my ten-year-old son and two other boys for target practice on their way out."

"What about the law?"

"Gracious, those kind of killers didn't sit down in Kansas and hold their hands out to be handcuffed." She folded her arms over her breasts and sat up straight. "Kansas law said they'd get them, but you and I both know that's just so much talk. They're gone, long gone to Hades or somewhere else."

"And you're going up against five killers?" He shook his head mildly in disbelief. No way.

"Four. I blew one apart in the store with a shotgun, and I also got some lead in the leader."

"Three and a half killers would make short work of you."

She ignored his words. "They killed my husband and son. And that's why I'm here to hire you."

"You have any names for these men?"

With a sharp nod, she wet her lips and began. "Charlie Bowdry, he's the boss, Nickel Malloy, he's the kid. Henny Williams and Indian Tee."

"Colonel Charles Bowdry?" Slocum shook his head and looked at the gray boards under his dusty boots. He'd had a run-in with the big man—Galveston, Texas, a long time ago—over Bowdry slapping some dove around. He'd made him stop doing it, and only the law arriving saved a gun-fight.

"You know him?" she asked with a glint of hope in her eyes.

"He ain't exactly a favorite of mine. Former Confederate captain who raised his own rank to colonel. Been in some scraps with the law. Supposedly robbed a couple of banks, stole a few herds of cattle, but did that in the Nation, so he was under Fort Smith law and Judge Parker's U.S. marshals never caught him."

"You know any of the others?"

Slocum shook his head. "May recognize them when I see them."

"Here." She raised herself to fish out some folded wanted posters from her pants pocket, and eased back down. She flattened out the first one on the bench seat. "The kid. Nickel Malloy alias Morgan Davis."

"Wanted for murder of two federal black troopers in Waco," he read off the poster. "Two-fifty reward."

"That's the short list on him. This next guy here is a skinny-looking cowboy," she said, topping the first with another sheet. "Henny murdered his wife, and two other women they know about."

Slocum pursed his lips and gave her a wry look. "Real nice bunch."

"Indian Tee, also known as Black Knife. Wanted for murder, rape and robbery by Arkansas authorities."

He folded his arms over his vest, slumped down on the bench, crossed his outstretched legs at the ankles with a ring of his spur rowels and shook his head. "And you're going after them?"

"Yes, I came to hire you to help me."

"Lady, them four men could whip up on a good posse."

"We need a posse, I'll hire them."

"You're talking big bucks, real big bucks." He stared at his scuffed boot toes. This would never work—she wasn't tough enough in the first place. Some housewife dressed in drover's clothing, packing a .32 short-barreled Colt on her hip. It'd never work.

"Those—those men killed my husband, they killed my son. They can't hide forever, and when those vermin stick their heads up out of some hole, I aim to blow them off. Now, you can help me or not. I won't rest till they're all dead." Impatience glaring on her smooth face, she started to get up.

"Or they kill you." He put his hand on her arm to stay her. "Mrs.—"

"Wink's my name."

"Wink, go back to that store. Stay busy. Post some rewards for them."

"I rode a fur piece to get here and find you. Jim Bob said you were my man. I guess he misjudged you."

He closed his eyes, pushed his stiff shoulders against the back of the bench and slow-like shook his head. She didn't understand the hard nature of what she proposed. About then, two cowboys reined up and dismounted; he gave a head bob to them.

Both blinked in surprise once they were in the porch's shade and out of the glare and realized the person seated beside him was a good-looking woman. They fumbled to remove their hats for her and half stumbled over the threshold looking back.

Amused, Slocum about laughed at their obvious frustration, then, serious, he turned back to her. "Go back, go back to the store."

Her eyes narrowed and she looked away, taking in the passing buckboard. "Can't. I sold everything I owned."

"Go back to your kin—at home."

"Don't have any kin. My family was killed over ten years ago in an Indian raid. Those four bastards killed my only family."

He drew his boots up and stamped the floorboards. "Then we need to get you in shape for this ordeal."

"In shape? What do you mean 'in shape'?"

"Can you run a mile?"

"I don't know, never had to."

"Chasing down killers is tough, hard work for a man, be twice as hard on a woman."

"What do I need to do to prove to you—" Her even white teeth were clenched tight and her stare was cold as a northerner.

"When you can run a mile and not get out of breath, shoot a tin can four out of six times and lift a hundred pounds— we'll go find those killers."

"But they may—"

"Get killed by someone else? Be good riddance, right?"

"Where are we going to do all this?"

"I got a friend down in the Nation, Hurricane Wilson. We can stay at his place."

"What—what's he?"

Slocum looked at the distorting heat waves that rose off the waving dry grass in the vacant prairie across the street. "An old Cherokee outlaw turned medicine man."

"We really need to go to—him?" The edge of her voice sounded uncertain.

"Wink, that's what they call you?"

"Yes, for Winkle."

"If you're planning on going after men like the colonel, Hurricane Wilson will be like a Baptist preacher compared to the creatures you'll meet on their trail."

"You're trying to scare me out of this. I won't be." She folded her arms over her breasts and sulked on the bench.

"Good. Let's ride to Wilson's." He stood up and stretched.

"How far away is he?"

"Depends."

"On what?" She frowned at him.

"Whether you can fly like an eagle or ride a horse. Eagles will get there faster."

"Where's your horse?"

"Livery yard, I'll go get him."

"Meanwhile I'll get some things from the store for us to eat on the way." She tossed her head in that direction.

"Three days' worth. Should be there by then." He started to leave and appraised her as she strode for the doorway. Willowy figure, she looked interesting enough under the cowboy garb. Time would sure tell. He drew a deep breath and stepped off the porch—Lord only knew how this would turn out.

He moved under the blazing midday sun toward the sign marked "Livery Yard. Good Horses For Sale." That place hadn't sold a good horse since Columbus landed from Spain. When he'd arrived there two days before, he'd looked over the wind-broke plugs in the corral—none of them would make it ten miles before collapsing.

The whiskered owner came to the office door chewing on a straw. "Ya leaving already?"

"Yep, can't find a Delmonico steak in any of the fancy cafés here."

The man chuckled. "Hell, last two days, you've won enough playing cards to start a café of your own."

Slocum nodded and closed his eyes to the too bright sun's glare. "Trouble is now there ain't any rich enough customers left around here for my menu."

The man tossed the straw away. "Give you fifty and a good horse for that dun you're riding."

"Naw, me and ole Dunny got to move on."

"With that good-looking bitch come by here looking for you?"

Stung by his words, Slocum pushed past the man and inside the office. "What do I owe you?"

"Buck and a half."

Slocum dug the money out of his vest pocket, switched the coins to his left hand and held out his closed fist to drop them into the expectant palm. When the man's attention went to the falling silver, Slocum hit him with a right cross and sent him on his ass.

"Next time, don't mix dogs up with ladies."

"Hell, you didn't need to get mad about it." He sat on his butt and rubbed his jaw. "Make it seventy-five and I ain't going a dime higher."

Saddle and bridle in his hands, Slocum turned back, going out the stable side door to get his horse. "Not for sale."

The dun under pad and saddle, he led him outside and prepared to mount. The liveryman stood hatless in the doorway, still feeling his jaw. "Ninety bucks and that's robbery."

With a shake of his head, Slocum mounted and never looked back. Wink was coming out of the store with two cotton pokes of things when he reined up before her. He smiled and she held up one for him.

"What all did you buy?" He took it from her.

Busy tying her cotton sack on the horn, she looked back at him. "Jerky, crackers, dry cheese and some airtight tins of peaches and tomatoes. I use to help run a store; I know what drifters like."

Slocum chuckled and turned the dun back east. No telling, she might be lots of fun yet. When they rode past, he nodded to the liveryman, who watched them with an eagle eye from his doorway. Then an older man drove past them in a buckboard, on his way to town; he looked grouchy and in a big hurry. Slocum swung Dunny south, wide of the last small frame house, and she kept her roan horse close to his.

He took in how she rode—natural, which amazed him. Part of the horse and saddle, not like he'd thought, her being a storekeeper's wife—widow. He had expected her to plow-pull the roan around with too much rein or choked up short in fear it'd run off.

"Where did you learn how to ride?"

"I always rode horses—till I married Walter. He never kept one."

"How old did you get married?"

"Fourteen."

His gaze on the line of hills in the south, he nodded. "You said something about a wagon train raid?"

"Oh, yes, everyone in our wagon train was killed. I managed to get away going for help. But I was too late."

He twisted in the saddle and looked at her. "Indians?"

"Of course. Who else raids wagon trains?"

"Lots of those raids were done by white men and the Indians got the blame."

She looked hard at him. "I never thought of that. My entire family was murdered and two other families too that made up the train. Walter was a widower. He took me in after the funeral and decided we should get married—it would look bad otherwise, me being of age and all."

"You had children?"

"A boy, the next year—Tobias—" She looked away,

"I guess you and Walter got along."

"Dutiful," she said.

"I savvy that."

"He wasn't cruel to me. I'm embarrassed to say it, but I expected something more I guess from a marriage. Still, he did take me in."

"Yes." No big deal he could see for some older man to take in an attractive girl and make her his wife, but she appreciated the man for it, which showed lots of character to Slocum. "Let's lope a ways. There's creek ahead that might have some water in it and we can rest the horses there."

She nodded and set the roan in a high lope. He looked back and saw nothing but a few buzzards searching in big arcs on an updrift. Wink was sure a funny name for a woman. He sent Dunny flying after her.

What the hell would that old Cherokee medicine man think of her? He'd like her.

2

"That water looks absolutely inviting," she said as their horses shifted back and forth, going down the steep decline toward the final high bank, both animals sweaty and breathing hard.

"Guess you could swim in that hole over there." He pointed through the gnarled trunks of the tall, rustling cottonwoods at an inviting blue pool.

She nodded, looked around and then back at him. "Guess we're alone, ain't we?"

"Yes, ma'am, why?"

"I figured part of my test today is, can she swim?"

He nodded, swallowing his amusement.

"Well, Slocum. I can swim better than most damn fish." And she swung her leg over the cantle. The roan tied to some sapling, she jerked loose the gunbelt and hung it on the horn. On the far side of her horse, she ignored him and began to unbutton the blouse and then to hang it over the gun. Then she undid a money belt to hang over the gun set and next toed off her boots. All he could see was her bare shoulders and shining hair showing above the saddle's seat, as she undid and shed her pants next and hung them up.

"Guess you've seen lots of naked women before," she said and started down the steep bank for the water using a bush or two for support. At last on the edge, with a quick look back up at him that showed off the long, brown-capped breasts, she smiled uneasy-like and dove in.

He gathered her clothing, boots, money belt and gun, then carried them down the high bank to the water's edge. Never a bad idea to have them close in case she needed them. He left the horses to graze on top. Squatted down on his boot heels at the side of the pool, chewing on a bluestem stalk, he watched her through the glinting sunlight take long strokes through the water. Downstream, she rose up with her hands to her eyes and fought the wet hair back. Liquid ran down her shapely white body, and she swept the curls back from her face to blink at him.

"Come on in. It's wonderful."

"Bet it is. But if one of the colonel's men caught you that far from your gun, what would happen?" He could tell his words had taken her aback. She folded her arms and bit her lip, stamping her bare heel on the ground without an answer.

Then she rubbed her palms on the top of her snowy legs. "It won't happen ever again, teacher."

"Good," he said and stood up to toe off his boots.

She dove in and dog-paddled toward that side of the hole. "Damn you, Slocum. You tricked me."

Undoing his shirt, he laughed as he pulled it off over his head. "Not like they would."

Undressed, he took his time wading out to the hole. She was in the water up to her neck, looking away. He advanced until he reached knee-deep, tepid water, and then dove in for a swim. It must be spring-fed, he decided, making powerful strokes—the liquid turned cooler out in the current flowing through the hole.

He came up waist-deep on the far side and wiped his face.

"I thought I'd shock you doing that," she said, in a small voice. "Getting naked, I mean. I wanted to prove to you, I'll do anything to get those killers."

He nodded. "I imagine you will." He backstroked away from her. "Can you shoot?"

"I used to shoot a .22."

"Good. You say you shot one of them in the robbery?" He was barely stroking, only enough to stay up, and watching intently for her answer.

"Walter, my husband, kept a shotgun under the counter. After they killed him, I crept over there and shot a Mexican coming up the aisle with it."

"What next?"

"The recoil spilled me on the floor, and they shot the shelves of airtight cans to pieces over me. Whew, I was soaked in peach and tomato juice. But I got up and then winged the colonel. They left after that."

He found his feet and stood up. "I'm not shocked at your wanting to prove yourself. I know you want these men, but why did they kill your son?"

"That neighbor boy who was with him and lived said the kid—Malloy, whoever—rode up where they were in the creek wading after frogs and said, 'Boys, let's see who can shoot the best.' Then they opened fire on them."

"Tough bunch of no-accounts."

She nodded and then a serious look spread over her face. "Can I swim good enough to suit you?"

He nodded and laughed. "Yes, ma'am, and it ain't bad scenery."

Her face turned red and she started to leave.

"Aw, you better stay in here and enjoy this while we can. We still have two days' ride left to get to Hurricane's."

She nodded and eased down to swim some more. Turning back, she laughed uneasily. "No wife? No home? No roots?"

"None of that."

"Billy Bob said they wanted you in Kansas? What for?"

"Long time ago—a kid came after me with a gun in a saloon. It was self-defense. But his family owned the law in Fort Scott, and they've kept two deputies on my heels ever since."

"Couldn't you—"

"No, they own the law. I'm the outsider. Never get a fair trail."

"Whew, I thought I had troubles."

He met her face-on and she struggled for moment to find her footing. Water ran off her quaking, firm breasts and, her blue eyes opened wide, she rose to her feet. With her upper arms in his hands, he bent over and kissed her.

At first, her lips were frozen. Then as if awoken from some long sleep, she threw her arms around his neck; he hugged her tight to him and her lips parted for his tongue. When at last they broke their mouths away, she huffed for her breath wrapped in his arms.

"Did I shock you?" he asked—but before she could answer, he heard something and whirled around, but couldn't see the source of the sounds for the high dirt bluff above them.

"What's wrong?" she whispered.

"Someone's stealing our horses," he said, and started through the waist-deep water for his gun.

3

Eagles would have been quicker, Slocum decided. The old wagon the two of them rode in pounded over every rut, rock and bump in the twin tracks through the brown grass. The Cheyenne woman on the seat driving it must be looking for bumps to run over, he decided, seated on his butt in back. He'd hired Yellow Deer to haul them to Hurricane's after they'd walked two days on foot.

Lucky for them the horse thieves didn't get their clothing, guns, boots and one sack of groceries spilled in their haste to run off. All he saw reaching the top of the bluff was two riders leading off their mounts in a high lope going north like their pants were afire. Damn them anyway.

Seated beside him in the wagon bed, Wink reached over and clamped his larger, calloused hand in hers and smiled at him. "Guess this was another test, huh?"

"Those damn horse thieves are going to think it's a test if I ever catch them."

"How did they ever track us there?"

"That damn livery man back there must have sent them. He offered me a horse and ninety bucks for the dun. Wanted him bad."

"And I was just getting used to that snorty roan."

"Hurricane can get us some more."

She raised up and looked over the country. "We getting close?"

"We'll be there by sundown."

"Good. My backside's sore." She squirmed and made a face. "Guess that gets tough too."

"Ain't no goose-down seat." He laughed and hugged her shoulder. "But it shows you what can happen even when you aren't chasing killers."

"I sure never slept on the ground before without a blanket."

"All kinds of inconvenience that the loss of one's horses causes. Gives you an idea how neat it is to be on the run."

"I can't say I'd love that—"

"Lawmen coming," Yellow Deer said, over her shoulder, above the pound of her horses' hooves, the jingle of harness and the squeak of the wheels and wagon.

Slocum rose on his knees and hung on to the back of the spring seat to better judge the two men with rifles across their laps, riding toward them on the ruts cut through the dry grass. Both men wore brown business suits and narrow-brim cowboy hats, and jig-trotted good horses toward them.

"What do they want?" Wink asked, looking unsure of this business at hand.

"Look for whiskey," Yellow Deer said and slapped her right horse for lagging.

"Well, we don't have any of that," Wink said, sounding relieved.

"What do you think's in them crates?" He gave a head toss to the wooden boxes on the other side of the wagon bed from where they sat.

"Oh, no."

"Don't say a word."

"Fine." She swallowed hard, looking wary. "I sure won't."

"Ho! Ho!" Yellow Deer drew back the leather reins and halted the coughing horses.

"Well, Yellow Deer, you doing stage line business now?"

the marshal with the snowy mustache asked with a smile as he dismounted and came over to her.

"Stole their horses," she grunted.

"You got any illegal whiskey today?"

Then she nodded with a look of disgust and reached in her quilted bag on the floor. From it she handed him a pint of opened whiskey and dug out twenty dollars to give to him.

"Caught you again," the lawman said, looking at the bottle and money in his hand. "You know you can't bring whiskey into the Nation."

She nodded woodenly, looking straight ahead.

His partner, holding the other officer's horse, bobbed his head in agreement from the saddle. "We get you every time."

"I didn't catch your name," the marshal on the ground said to Slocum. "I'm Hap Gaines and that's Will Martin, deputy U.S. marshal for Judge Parker's Court in Fort Smith, Arkansas.

"Tom White and my missus, Wanda. Stole our horses back in Kansas and we're hitching a ride to go buy some more. Got to get back to Texas."

"Mrs. White." He removed his hat for her. "I am truly sorry about the loss of your horses. This world is full of crooks anymore."

"Yes, it must be," she said and thanked him, taking her seat again on the wagon floor beside Slocum.

"Have a good day, ma'am. And, Yellow Deer, stop trying to bring whiskey into the Nation. We're watching for you."

"You watch 'em too gawdamn good," she said, sounding mad. She clucked to her horses then drove them around Martin to get under way again.

The marshal waved his hat at Wink, and Slocum smiled when he knew the man could no longer see him.

"What about the rest of this whiskey?" she whispered, frowning at the cases at their feet.

"She paid her fine, gave him the evidence, a half-drunk pint of whiskey, and they get to keep it as well as the on-the-spot fine money. Arresting her and taking her to Fort Smith would mean several days' travel and only a dollar for her arrest. They aren't liable to search too hard then, are they?"

"So she's paid the taxes on this load, you're saying?"

"Sure has. They do that every time?" he asked Yellow Deer.

"Every time unless big man is up here. I usually get word and don't go up there for whiskey until him goes back to Fort Smith. Him mean sumbitch put Crazy George in jail for doing it. Got him one year in Detroit prison for bringing in firewater. Only give Belle Star nine months and she stole a gawddamn horse."

"Good idea you avoid the big man." He turned back to Wink. "It's called live and let live."

"I'm learning, lots," Wink said and stretched her arms over her head. "Glad that is over."

Rocked back and forth by the wagon's roll, he agreed. But it would be even better to be at Hurricane's—the day was dragging on. He checked the blazing sun time, still five hours away from there by his calculations. At least they weren't walking the last ten miles.

Several tall cottonwoods shaded the corrals, sod-roofed shed and low-walled cabin with smoke coming out the chimney. All the operation sat painted a burning orange color in the canted light of sundown. Dogs barking and a few loose, weaned pigs made a trail to cover in a long lope. One of Hurricane's studs whistled and kicked at his pen as if impatient for a mare to breed. A couple of Jersey milk cows bawled for their calves separated from them.

"Ho! Ho!" Yellow Deer shouted, reining her arms back till her elbows hit the seat back and the team stopped.

Slocum unfolded and rose in the wagon box. "Thanks, Deer."

He helped Wink up and steadied her on her feet—shaky from sitting for so long. He slipped off the tailgate, and then she sat on the back edge to get off, and when she jumped he caught her in his arms.

"We're here?" she asked as he set her down.

He looked around. "I hope so."

"See you 'gain," Yellow Deer said, not looking, and sending her horses on with a wave.

Wink laughed. "She didn't wait around long."

Slocum nodded.

"Well, who in the hell she drop off here?" a dark-complected, short man with a thin salt-and-pepper mustache asked, looking around when he came outside putting up his galluses, then spying them.

"That you, Slocum?" The man looked worried as he rushed over. "Where's your horses?"

"They stole them up in Kansas three days ago."

"Well, gawdamn, I'd come got you."

"Your telegraph is down."

"I guess so, and who is she?" He drew his bare head back and studied her with his arms folded.

"Mrs. Trent; they call her Wink. Colonel Bowdry and his men shot her husband and son in a robbery of their store up there."

"Oh, golly, I am sorry," Hurricane said and took her hands in his. "Then someone stole your horses?"

"It's been a very educational time." She made a smile for the man who looked so concerned about her.

"I am so glad you came." His attention centered on her.

"I am too," she said, sounding grateful.

"Things will be better here, right, Slocum?"

"That's why we came here. It had to get better." The three laughed, and Hurricane led them to the front door and opened it slow-like.

In the dim lamplight in the room, Slocum saw past him into the room as a dusky-skinned, naked girl on the bed threw off the covers and bounded away. Hurricane closed the door and wrinkled his nose. "She must have thought it was bedtime. She'll be dressed in a minute."

When they came inside the cabin, the Indian girl was wiggling down the dress and her large brown eyes raised up and looked hard at them.

"My friends," Hurricane said to her. "That is Mrs.—"

"Wink," she corrected him, and stuck out her hand to the shapely teenager with high cheekbones and coal black hair.

"Her name is Blue Bird. I call her Blue."

"Nice to meet you, Blue," Wink said and shook her hand.

"He's Slocum."

Blue nodded to him.

"Heat them some food," Hurricane said and turned back to Slocum. "Who stole your horses?"

"Don't know, we were swimming," Slocum said, taking a wooden chair he offered them.

"Hmm," Hurricane snuffed out his nose.

"They would have gotten our clothing and guns, but he brought them down to the water," Wink said. "I'm learning."

"Good teacher." Hurricane nodded in approval.

"We need to buy two good saddles and horses and need a place to stay for a couple of weeks."

"Sure. We can find them and you two can stay here."

Slocum nodded and then looked hard at his old friend. "I told her she needed to get tough to go after the colonel."

Hurricane agreed with a slow nod and gave her a serious look across the table. "Need to be plenty gawdamn tough you go after him."

"I can do it."

Hurricane nodded as if considering her words.

Blue interrupted them, handing out tortoise bowls and spoons, then went back for her cast iron pot. A rag pot holder around the loop handle, she ladled the bean soup out into each bowl with a nod. Slocum sampled the soup and nodded. "It's sure good. We've had tomatoes and peaches for two days."

Everyone laughed.

After the meal, Hurricane showed them to a small board-sided shed with a bed and loaned them two old blankets. Slocum lighted a candle that Blue had given him. The two were alone at last. She sat on the edge of the bed and tested its stiffness with her butt. The flickering light cast huge shadows of them on the walls.

Slocum, weary from the long ride, was seated on a wooden crate as he took off his boots. "Sorry about all this happening—the horse stealing and all."

"No—don't be. It's taught me a real important lesson. I need to think about everything. Not simply the moment."

"Good."

She stood up and began to undress, then stopped undoing the buttons on her shirt to look at him. "You started something back there in Kansas you never finished."

"Oh, yah." A smile swept over his face at the consideration, and he nodded as the blouse gaped open, exposing the brown rosettes of her nipples. "Where was I?"

She undid the money belt and pulled it out to drop on the floor, then stepped over and put her arms around his neck when he rose. "Something like this—"

His mouth closed on hers, and this time she was ready. Her wet lips parted, and she clung to him as his hand sought her right breast. His fingers gentle squeeze drew a gasp from her in response to his molding the tight-skinned boobs. She moved her hip against his leg. The shirt slid off her shoulders as his lips and tongue sought her hot mouth. She fought between them to undo his gunbelt and then ripped open his pants. In her rush, she shoved the galluses off his shoulders and then gasped holding his half-turgid dick in both hands.

"Oh, my God." She closed her eyes, squeezing it tight.

He undid her pants and pushed them off her hips. She fought the legs off, kicking them free, and dropped to the bed, letting go of him as she situated herself in the middle of the mattress on her back. Arms lifted for him, she looked pale-faced in the flickering light.

He needed no more encouragement than that. His hips ached to plunge deep inside her. At last, on his knees, he crossed the spongy bed and guided his throbbing rod for her target. The swollen head slipped in the slick gates and butted against the tight ring. He felt her hands grip his upper arms that were braced on the bed on each side of her as he pumped against the resistance. Then the nose of his prick began to press open the way, and she raised her hips to ease his entry with a sharp cry. His huge erection began to fill the void as he drove deeper and deeper with each effort.

In pleasure's deepest involvement, moaning and tossing her head, with her curls spilling in her face, she gasped for more air. He moved in and out as the walls tightened in her heightened response. Her erect clit tore at the top of his dick, driving both of them wilder and wilder. Sweat greased their bellies, and they ground the coarse hair between them on their pubic bones. It was harder and deeper with each plunge, until she cried out and braced for the end—and he came from deep and exploded out of the bottom of his testicles. His final effort was a charge that flooded her.

When he rose off of her, he blew out the light and then settled in beside her. He moved the hair aside from her face with his fingertips, raised himself up on one arm and kissed her. "You all right?"

"No. My God, I was married eleven years and never had anything like that happen before." She put the back of her hand to her forehead. "I'm so dizzy, I feel I'll roll out of bed."

"Going to be sick?"

She turned, then rose to get over him, jammed a hard breast in his chest, and laid her forehead on him. "Somehow I knew there was more to this than what I'd experienced. But—oh—I never expected that to happen. It was like I was falling off a mountain and then whoosh I was unconscious."

She squirmed in a stretch on top of him. Her right hand rubbed the corded muscles of his lower stomach as if exploring for something, combed the nest of hair, and then she hefted his half-full erection as if weighing it.

She laughed aloud at her discovery. "He's not half-dead yet. God rest his soul, poor Walter had ever in his life been that big he'd've busted his buttons."

His mind fast coming on to trying it again with her, he cupped her face and kissed her hard on the mouth. "Then for his sake, we better do it again, huh?"

"Really? I may never walk again."

He wrinkled his nose in the dim light of the shack. "I'll carry you then."

"You've got a deal."

4

"Porter may have some horses for sale," Hurricane said over breakfast the next morning.

"They stolen?" Slocum asked, taking two more of Blue's baking soda biscuits and splitting them on his plate. He spooned some of her thick flour/sausage gravy over them and set in to devour it. "Good food, Blue." And turned back to Hurricane.

"Naw, he's honest."

"We don't need stolen horses. Some law pick up on it and we'd have a hard time explaining. Ain't got time for that."

Her face wringing wet with perspiration, Wink hung her head inside the doorway, out of breath, and looked at him for orders. "I ran around the place ten times."

"Good," Slocum said and wiped his mouth on his kerchief. "Better wash up and eat. Target practice is next."

Still breathing hard, she nodded woodenly. "I'll wash up out here first." Then she went back to deep breathing outside on the porch.

"You got an old .45?" Slocum asked his host.

"Why so big?" Hurricane asked in a low voice.

"Build her muscles. I'll pay for the cartridges. You can hit

28

a bull in the ass with a .45—you can shoot his eye out with a .32 later."

"I wasn't worried about the ammo. You're going to kill her."

"Better I take the fight out of her than Bowdry." With his fork, Slocum cut another bite off the gravy-smothered biscuit.

"He'd kill her."

"That's what I mean."

"You want some coffee?" Hurricane asked, when Wink sat down hard on the chair he proffered.

"Oh," Wink said absently, still trying to recover her composure. "Sure."

"I'm going to set up some targets for you while Hurricane and I go look at some horses today," Slocum told her.

Numb-like, she nodded to Blue, who poured her some coffee. "Okay—what else?"

"Get through, you take the gun apart. Clean it in boiling water, dry it, then lightly oil every part of it."

"I never took a gun apart before." Blue brought her some fired eggs, side meat and biscuits. "Thanks. Can I hurt it?"

"If it's not loaded, no."

"Good," she sighed. "I won't clean it loaded, trust me."

"You can quit firing when you get five out of six bullets in a quarter-sized newspaper sheet."

"What distance?"

Slocum laid down his fork and chewed on his mouthful. "Thirty feet to start."

Hurricane came back and put an older model Colt, modified for cartridges, on the table with two boxes of shells beside it. She tried to heft it and was forced to use both hands. "Damn, this is a heavy gun."

"It might be the only gun available for you to use between your life and death," Slocum said, finishing his biscuit-and-gravy dessert.

She nodded and began to eat.

Hurricane was cutting up old newspaper pages into fourths. "We got lots of targets."

Wink nodded, "I may need them all."

Half an hour later, holding the Colt in both hands, she aimed at the target. The muzzle exploded and the black powder smoke swept back in her face, causing her to cough. She dropped her gun hand down and turned her head aside.

"Did I hit it?"

"No, you can't shut your eyes and shoot."

"All right—this ain't going to be easy, you knew that?"

"I knew you said you could do it."

A grim set to her jaw and tight-pressed lips, she took aim despite her wet eyes. "And I will." Next three shots, one even hit the paper.

With a nod for her to continue, he mounted the bay horse he'd borrowed from Hurricane and they rode out the gate. The older man riding a red mule, they headed for a place called Soda Gap. This man Porter there dealt in *un-stolen* horses. Hard to find in the Nation, Hurricane informed him. They crossed the windswept, bluestem-clad, rolling country, keeping to the high rims. Hurricane wore an unblocked hat complete with eagle feather and a quilted vest with the Cherokee star on his back despite the day's growing warmth.

"Is he going to be home—this guy Porter we're going to see?"

"Yes."

"How do you know?"

"A bee told me so."

Slocum nodded. If a bee's information was good enough for Hurricane, it was good enough for him. "You act kind of stiff today?"

"I'll be fine." The older man grinned. "It is work to make a young woman happy in bed. Maybe I outdid myself." Then he laughed aloud. "I am glad you came. I worried something had happened to you—maybe because they stole your horses. I just knew all was not well with you."

"I've been healthy." Slocum shrugged off his friend's concern.

"Not that, but bad spirits have been stalking you."

"What can I do about them?"

"Smoke some special tobacco I have mixed for you."

"Will that cure them?" He reined the bay off a long hill toward the tree-lined watercourse that snaked through a flat, grassy valley dotted by scattered homesteads.

"If my medicine is stronger than theirs." Hurricane chuckled, moving his mule in closer.

"If I showed you some posters of the men killed her husband and son, would you know if it was them?"

Hurricane nodded slowly. "Maybe, if it is them."

"She has the posters. I'll show them to you when we get back."

"Good, I will look at them. Here." He handed Slocum some papers to roll a cigarette.

Slocum took one and handed him the rest back ruffled by the growing wind. He exchanged the papers for a small leather sack. His back turned to shield his efforts from the forces, he filled the V-shaped paper with the fine shredded tobacco, then pulled the small sack's drawstring tight using his teeth. Hurricane took the pouch back and Slocum twisted the cylinder tight. With the tip of his tongue he licked it shut. Then, holding his head to the side and the cigarette in his lips, he struck a match from his vest and began to drag on it. The sweet smoke soon filled his mouth and he inhaled it.

Powerful stuff, he decided, exhaling.

"Porter's place is that one over there." Hurricane pointed to the southwest.

Slocum nodded and tried another puff. He sure hoped the medicine worked—all he needed was more trouble than the colonel and his killers. Maybe she would stay with Blue and Hurricane while he went to find them—doubtful. Time would only tell. He sure hoped this Porter had some decent horses.

A short man came out of the frame house to meet them. Definitely not an Indian, he wore a starched white shirt with pressed wool pants. Porter was in his fifties, and when he swept the windblown dark hair back from his face, he looked like a man of wealth. Something about his manners and dress said he was also a lady's man

"How've you been, Hurricane?" he asked as they dismounted.

"Fine, fine, Porter, that's Slocum, he needs two horses. Someone stole his up in Kansas."

"Nice to meetcha." They shook hands. "Damn thieves are bad along the border. They duck the law going back and forth. What did they steal?"

"A stout blue roan, probably came out of old Mexico, and a sure enough good dun horse with an MC brand on his right shoulder."

"I'll watch for them. But they don't bring a lot of stolen ones to me."

"Good, thanks. I'd turned down a hundred bucks for the dun."

Porter nodded and turned to shout at someone unseen. "Boy, go bring in those horses."

A young Indian holding a pitchfork came out of the barn and nodded at him. In a second he was gone inside and reappeared ducking his head to get outside, riding a leggy gray mare bareback. He swung open the gate and loped off down the bottom to gather them.

"Where do you live?" Porter asked.

"Looking for a place," Slocum said, and the answer was accepted.

Heads high, the horses came in. From big feather-legged draft horses to stout cow ponies, they milled in the yard. The boy busied himself cutting out the work horses and some others, and sending them back to pasture.

"How about the big stout horse?" Porter pointed out the tall black horse in the bunch.

"He looks good, but I'd like to see some of those Texas ponies up close." He didn't need a conspicuous horse like the black to draw attention to him and Wink.

"Those ponies came from John Blocker, Texas cattle dealer."

"I know Blocker. Took some herds up the trail for him."

"I bought those in Abilene last summer. Boys all went to

Chicago on the train and he had no one to take them back."

"Let's catch that sorrel and the bay with the snip."

"Boy," he shouted to the youth and then listed the ones he wanted.

A bob of the brown face and he kicked the gray into action. In minutes, he brought up the sorrel and handed the lead to Porter.

"Good help," Slocum said, putting his hand on the gelding's neck and talking to him. He bent over and checked his front hoof, and dropped it when he was satisfied it was sound. He did the same on the back two and the other front. Then he mouthed him for six years old.

Complete, he forced the pony backward. That worked, so he moved out to look him over, and satisfied, he turned back to Porter. "How much?"

"Fifty bucks."

"Thirty-five. You must have given Blocker ten for them."

"You know about the deal?"

Slocum shook his head. "I know Blocker. He cut his losses and gave them to you."

"You wanted two, here's the second one." The boy led him up and piled off the gray, handing Slocum the lead.

Nice-looking dark bay, a little dish-faced and high-headed, but stylish enough for her to ride. He found him sound and probably five years old. The dickering began, and Porter had several used saddles and Navajo saddle pads to choose from.

Two hours later, the three men ate lunch at the kitchen table with Porter's Indian wife, Nonia, and Slocum savored her good fry bread. The sale had been made for one hundred twenty-five bucks for the two outfits and both men had shaken hands on the deal. So, after the noon meal, Slocum rode the sorrel and led the other two, and with Hurricane on his mule, they headed back.

About to cross a long hogback, Hurricane stopped him. "Better go around."

"You see something?"

"No."

"A bee tell you?"

Hurricane nodded and booted his mule northward to avoid the high rise. Slocum looked back and saw nothing out of place on the grassy-covered knob, but he wasn't chancing Hurricane's prophecy or a bee's advice—better safe than sorry.

They reached Hurricane's place in mid-afternoon, and Wink acted pleased about her bay. Slocum got on him first, and he humped his back some riding him around, but never really bucked. When she got on him, he acted like a well-broke one.

A small Indian in his twenties rode up on a thin piebald horse and nodded to them. Knowing he wanted to speak to Hurricane, Slocum pointed to the house. The thin-faced man bobbed his head and rode on.

"What's he want?" she whispered.

"Guess to see Hurricane."

"He looked mean."

Slocum shook his head. "No, he wore no gun and had no rifle."

"They carry them when they're mad?"

"It helps."

"I won't forget that."

"Good. Did you have a nice day?" he asked her

"Yes, you know how old Blue is?"

"No."

"Fifteen, about the same age I was when I married Walter."

"She happy?"

"Oh, yes. She says she eats much better with him, and she—well—she really likes the being a wife part." Wink wrinkled her nose at him and then looked a little red-faced.

Laughing, he slung an arm over her shoulder, and they headed for the house. Target practice came again in the morning. He'd put the horses up later. Blue was signaling for them to come eat by waving her arm at them.

David Longthrow was the guest. Hurricane introduced him.

"David had a cow stolen." Hurricane explained.

"Recently?"

"Yesterday."

"He know who stole it?"

Both men nodded.

"What do we need to do?"

"The one who stole it is very tough."

"What should we do about that?" Slocum asked Hurricane.

"Go get his cow back for him." Then Blue interrupted her husband and he laughed. "Blue says we must eat first."

After supper, they decided to wait until dawn to ride over and confront the cow thief. Slocum went to put the horses up. Wink helped Blue with the dishes and heated water for them to sponge off before bedtime. Longthrow and Hurricane smoked on the porch and talked while the Susie bugs sizzled in the cottonwoods.

A night wind rustled the dollar-sized leaves, and somewhere down the valley a coyote cried at the rising quarter moon. Slocum had no idea about Hurricane's plan to recover the cow, but he intended to tag along and fill his hand if he needed him. The ponies in the pen and some hay forked in the manger, he headed for the open, lighted front door.

"May blow in some rain," Hurricane said when Slocum reached the porch.

Slocum looked around in the growing darkness. "Guess you can use it."

"Summertime, we can always use it. I'll wake you early."

"Fine whenever. Nice to meet you," he said to the other man.

"Yes."

He and Wink sponged off outside the back of the house in the starlight and dried with flour-sack towels. Feeling cleaner, he tossed out the pan of water while she lamented over how they couldn't wash their clothes too.

"I'll borrow his razor while they're still awake," he said, ready to go around in front.

"Good idea. They got yours in the saddlebags, didn't

they?" She fell in beside him. "My arm is sure sore. That old pistol is heavy."

"What was your best pattern?"

"You'll see in the morning."

"Maybe afternoon. I'm leaving early with Hurricane to see about the cow."

"You be careful doing that."

He chuckled. "I'm always careful." Always.

5

"You awake Slocum?" a voice in the darkness called to him.

"Yah, yah," he grunted, throwing his legs over the side and rubbing his sleep-hungry eyes in the darkness. "Be there in a few minutes."

"Good, she's got coffee and food."

Coming," he said and leaned over to kiss Wink on the ear.

She mumbled something back and like a groundhog going into her burrow, she pulled up the blankets to seek more sleep. He was up and dressing in the late night's coolness. Despite the day's heat, it had all evaporated and would start over the heating process the next day. Holding the Colt's cylinder to the stars' glow, he checked the loads and then, satisfied, holstered it. His hat on and silk kerchief around his neck, he stopped to empty his bladder and listen to the night sounds, a totally different orchestration than early night. Susie bugs asleep, a few crickets chirped and an owl hooted. A big one from the sounds of his bass voice and resounding "who"s.

He entered through the open cabin door and nodded to Hurricane and Longthrow seated at the table already eating breakfast in the candlelight. With a tin cup in his hand, he went to where Blue knelt before the fireplace, busy frying eggs in a skillet over the coals. The attractive girl smiled at him.

"Pretty damned early, ain't it?" he asked as she filled his cup.

"Maybe not pretty, but early," she said privately to him. They both laughed. "Here's your eggs," she said and put them on a china plate.

"Thanks." He rose with the plate in one hand and coffee in the other.

"Hear the owl hooting?" Hurricane asked.

Slocum put down his plate. "He a friend of yours?"

The older man nodded. "Good sign. He hasn't been around my house in a long time."

"Good," Slocum said, seated and reaching for the biscuits. Whatever that meant in Cherokee medicine.

"This guy who has David's cow is called Barrows," Hurricane offered. "He is a big bully."

"What will you do to him?"

Hurricane's brown eyes met his. "Maybe have to kill him."

"Whatever." Slocum busied himself with eating.

"Why would you even go with us—you're a white man?" Longthrow asked over his fork of scrambled eggs.

Slocum nodded and looked hard at him. "Hurricane's my friend. He asked me to go."

That must have satisfied the man, for he went back to eating without comment.

They saddled by starlight, and Slocum noticed that Hurricane carried a double-barrel shotgun. His red mule wringing his shorn tail, Hurricane set out with Longthrow on his thin horse and Slocum aboard the sorrel in the rear. Red, as he called him, acted halfway spooky at first, then settled into a long swinging walk. Be better when he'd been ridden some, especially after all his time turned out on pasture; horses always forgot something about being rode again.

Dawn was a gray flannel blanket behind the ragged clouds in the east when they rode off a ridge toward a dark set of buildings and pens. Hurricane stopped his mule and waved Slocum forward.

"You circle wide and come in from the east. Trouble starts, you can come on in."

"If he turns tail and runs, which way will he go?" Slocum gripped the horn and tried to loosen it—nothing gave—it was a good saddle.

"To you, I think."

"I'll be watching for him."

"He might shoot at you."

"He better have his best suit on if he does," Slocum said.

"Why?" Longthrow asked with a frown.

"It'll be what he's buried in if he shoots at me."

Both Cherokees chuckled. He smiled, nodded, then reined Red aside and went off though the stirrup-high bluestem that polished his boot toes.

A rooster crowed as he edged wide around the outfit. Somewhere a couple of hungry pigs squealed for food. Spears of sunlight came over his shoulder as he set Red up looking at the front door of the cabin in the distance. A couple of hounds went to raising hell, and soon Hurricane and Longthrow rode up to the hitch rack.

Hurricane called out to the cabin.

Someone appeared in the doorway in his pants and underwear top. Must be Barrows. The clatter of a rifle dropping from his hands carried to Slocum, who booted Red in closer. Hurricane had the shotgun's butt against his shoulder and pointed at the man in the doorway.

". . . came for David's cow," Hurricane spoke aloud as Slocum drew closer.

"His cow ain't here." Barrows filled the doorway with a red unbuttoned union suit and galluses hanging down, unshaven; he looked hard-eyed and mad.

"We want it," Hurricane insisted.

"I ain't got his gawdamn cow!"

"She's here in the barn," Longthrow said.

"Only cows in that barn are mine—you dumb son of a bitch!"

"Go get your cow," Hurricane said with a toss of his head.

The shotgun still ready in his hands, his dark face showed no sign of emotion.

Using his finger for a gun, Barrows pointed it at the man. "Longthrow, you take one of my gawdamn cows, I'll kill you! I know where you live."

"Get the cow!" Hurricane said louder when his man hesitated. "He won't bother you."

"You take one of my damn cows out of here, I'll cut your balls out, you little son of a bitch."

Longthrow put his hands to ears and ran toward the barn and pens.

"You better hear me!" Barrows said loud enough.

In a short while, Longthrow returned, leading a black-masked milk cow with curled horns. He looked like a frightened cur yard dog, but he led the cow up to the front of the house.

"This is my cow Sally. Has my ear notch on her right ear." He pointed to the long ago done job of marking her.

"Hogwash! I raised that cow!"

"Take her home, Longthrow," Hurricane said.

"You do—" The threat of the shotgun silenced his words spoken through gritted teeth,.

"Go on!" Hurricane frowned at Longthrow to make him move.

"I get my damn—"

The blast of Hurricane's shotgun caused Red to spook sideways, and Slocum had to catch the reins to check him. Through the cloud of acrid smoke, he saw Barrows lying on his back in the doorway. His bare feet stuck out on the porch and twisted in the throes of death. Screams from a woman inside began to reach a high pitch. Blood soon darkened Barrows' chest that smoldered from the burning gunpowder.

Hurricane shook his head in disapproval. "He should never have reached for that rifle."

He broke open the breech and took out a smoking shell. Longthrow was hurrying for his horse, leading the cow. As if still afraid, he glanced back once or twice and looked like the devil might be after him.

"Why did you shoot him?" the thick-waisted Indian woman screamed, standing over him.

" 'Cause he would never have let Longthrow alone."

Tears ran down her full cheeks and she nodded, solemn-like. "He would have killed him."

"Yes, now only one is dead." Hurricane gave a head toss to Slocum that he was ready to leave.

Slocum booted the sorrel in close, and when they were out of earshot, he asked, "That owl tell you to shoot him?"

Hurricane nodded, and the expression on his poker face never changed.

The first drops of rain struck Slocum, and he wished for the slicker they'd stolen from him. Cold as ice, the rain soon penetrated his shirt and drummed on his felt hat. Had the medicine man held it off that long? No telling. Thunder boomed in the west. More was coming.

6

"You have to bring the gun down, see the target and shoot," Slocum coached her, reaching around her to help support the heavy pistol in her hands. "Let's try again."

She raised the pistol, cocked it and made the downward arc—fired. The obvious hole in the newspaper target brought a shout from her and she twisted around to smile at him.

"See what I mean?"

"Yes, I do. I think I can handle it." She shuffled her boots to take the sideways stand he'd taught her earlier, to make less of a target. The pistol cocked, she made the arc and fired it.

"Good shot. Do it again."

"Yes, sir." With a deep inhale, the Colt rose again, cocked, and she brought it down and fired.

"That's three," he said and nodded in approval. "Reload."

"Why?"

"Always reload when you have the chance. Make it a habit; you might not get the chance again. I've seen men shoot five times and then get charged and killed because their opposition knew their gun was empty."

She nodded, shoving a fresh load in the gate.

"The toughest part is I can teach you how to shoot, but

42

facing a person and knowing you're going to kill him is tougher."

"It won't be for me," she said, replacing the last cartridge.

"We'll see."

"No," she said, twisting to face him. "I won't care. They shot my husband and son."

Slocum nodded and studied the windswept grassy hills. They'd see.

In two weeks, her running became natural and she hardly lost her breath circling the home place ten times. Her arms and shoulders grew more powerful lifting half-filled feed sacks for hours. She shot fifteen rounds every morning, and the targets were riddled with her bullets. In a bound, she could get on a bareback horse and be galloping away.

"Lots to this business," she said in his ear after they'd made fiery love in the bed later that night.

"Lots. I heard today that gang may be down in the Kiamish Mountains."

"Oh, when can we go after them?" Propped up on her elbows, in the starlight strained by the board siding of the shack, she appeared deep in thought.

"Oh, soon."

"How soon?"

His hand slid off her hip and he squeezed her rock-hard thigh under the thin shift. She raised up and kissed him. He rolled her over with his lips locked to her. In a flurry she raised her butt off the bed and pulled up the nightgown, spreading her legs apart. His recovering erection slipped in her slick gates and she gasped with pleasure as he drove it home. Her heels locked behind his knees, he began pumping it to her.

In minutes, she was deliriously lost in passion's throes, humping to his every stroke, wilder and wilder until the bed ropes creaked in protest underneath them. Her face was lost in the tossed curls and her mouth was open—gasping and moaning—until he reached under her, clutched both cheeks of her ass in his powerful grasp and in a hard, deep thrust fired his gun. She fainted.

7

In the soft light of predawn, Slocum finished tying down the diamond hitch over the gray pack mule that Hurricane gave them. Wink and Blue talked to the side as he readied to part with his friends. A coolness in the air reminded him fall wasn't far away. Shorter days. He'd planned all summer to winter in San Antonio—Kansas snowstorms held no appeal, nor did the Indian Nation's north wind that swept off the other's white stuff. High-breasted señoritas drumming on tambourines and dancing on the patios in the live oak–filtered sunshine were his idea of how to winter. Maybe he'd get there this time.

"Ready?" he asked, checking her cinch, then handing her the reins.

"Bye, Blue," she said over her shoulder, getting in the saddle.

The Indian girl ran over and looked up at her. "I will miss you, Wink."

"Heavens knows when I'll be back, but I'll come to see you if I am."

Blue nodded and pursed her dark lips. Lots of emotion in her sad eyes. Slocum turned back, shook Hurricane's hand and mounted up. It was not easy to leave those two.

He took the mule's lead and set out in a long trot. The Kiamish Mountains were a week away and a vast area to have to locate anyone. Choctaw and Seminole lands were in that region. He tried to catalog the people he knew down there and who might help them. Lots of outlaws in the land that would shoot you in the back over small change. Hardscrabble country with the riffraff of the entire state ending up where law came infrequently out of Fort Smith. Last grounds for many escaped and untried felons on the dodge from the law. Desperate men that would shoot it out rather than surrender. Mixed with breeds, full-blood renegades and ex-slaves. The area they sought was without God and civil niceties. Slocum looked aside at her—he hoped she was tough enough for the job.

They crossed the Canadian River on a ferry. A small pocket of clapboard shacks and false-front buildings hugged the south bank. When they reached the far side and led their animals off, tightening the cinch on Red, he heard her gasp. His hand went to his gun butt and he shoved Red aside. The first thing he saw was the white sole of a black's bare foot sticking almost into the road. A horde of flies sought the dead man's open eyes, nostrils and mouth.

"Hey," Slocum shouted at the ferryman. "There's a dead man over here."

"Yeah, that nigger's been dead a day or so."

He nodded to the concerned-faced Wink and then he spoke to the ferryman. "Ain't anyone going to do anything about him?"

The man mopped his neck with his red kerchief and shook his head. "Ain't my job."

"Any law here?"

"Naw."

"Thanks," Slocum said and tossed his head for her to mount up.

"We can't just—" Her face looked pale and close to tears; she gripped the saddle horn in her hand so tight her knuckles turned white.

"Ain't no one here to do it. I'll get a shovel and come back."

"Thanks," she said, relieved.

He pushed up the hill to the first store and dismounted. "Watch yourself. This place ain't two steps out of hell." Looking around, he mounted the steps and went though the open doors, seeing nothing out of place. The grit on the unswept floor ground under his boot soles and an unshaven man in a soiled apron looked up at his approach.

"Whatcha need?"

"Dead man up at the ferry. He belong around here?"

The man shook his head. "Just another dead nigger."

"He didn't live here?"

"Aw, he come from over at that settlement called Fish Camp."

"What was his name?"

"Jim Duncan."

"Who killed him?"

The man shrugged, not looking up, busy making scribbles on some butcher paper. "I don't know."

"Get me a ground cloth."

"Cost you seventy-five cents."

"I have the money, and a short-handled shovel too."

"That's another buck." He stretched and yawned openmouthed.

"You don't get your ass in gear, maybe there'll be a double funeral."

"You don't have to get touchy, I'm going. But I can tell you one thing."

"What's that?"

"You move that dead nigger, Frank Schade might not take it lightly."

"Why?" he said after the man's back as he moved to fill the order.

"You'll see. Frank Schade don't take to folks nosing into his business."

"He kill Duncan?"

"I don't know," the storekeeper said, laying the spade and sheet of canvas on the counter. "Buck seventy-five."

"You ain't very smart," Slocum said with an echo of irritation in his voice. "Where's Fish Camp?"

"Upstream a couple of miles; you can find plenty more of them lazy ones up there just like Duncan."

"That why he got shot?"

"Mister, with your attitude you won't last long around here."

"We'll see about that. What do they call this hog wallow?"

"Schadeville."

He gathered up his purchases. "Tell the mayor I took the body home."

"He'll find out fast enough."

Slocum never turned; he went out in the bright sun to where she sat in the saddle holding the horses and mule. Three young men were standing around her, and with their hats on the back of their heads, they looked like they came confidence-filled.

"Can I help you?" Slocum said, sharp enough that the straw-chewing one turned and grinned at him.

"All we want is a little pussy out of her—"

Without a blink, Slocum smashed him in the face with the spade and struck the second one in the gut so hard, his wind came out his O-shaped mouth. The third one fell over his boot heels backing up and, wide-eyed, scooted on his butt like a scorpion to escape Slocum's wrath. He finally made it to his feet and rushed off screaming about a madman.

"Which one of you's Frank Schade?" Slocum demanded.

"He ain't here," the one holding his bloody nose said.

"You tell him he better be careful. Killing blacks is as big a crime as killing whites in Judge Parker's court." Slocum swept up the ground cloth and handed it as well as the spade to Wink in exchange for his reins and the mule's lead rope.

"Thanks," she said under her breath.

A short bob of his head and he mounted. "Let's go get that body. He belongs at a place called Fish Camp."

She looked in disgust at the pair moaning on the ground, then booted her bay after him. He saw her shoulders quake with revulsion under the shirt.

"These folks in the Nation ain't polite cowboys like you met off the trail. They meant to rape you if you didn't go along with them."

"What should I have done?"

"Been ready to shoot them when they stepped in. If you'd hesitated, they'd've tore you off that horse and had their way with you."

She rubbed her left hand on the top of her pants leg as they trotted back to the ferry landing. "You said it wouldn't be easy."

"Could you have shot the first one?"

"I sure wasn't ready for that."

"You think about three studs poking you to death, you damn sure better think about killing the first one reached for you, anyway."

"I will," she said, reining up as he stopped and dismounted beside the corpse.

"Will what?" He looked hard at her for an answer.

A hard swallow and she nodded. "Blow them away like you said for me to do."

The body had begun to smell of death's putrefaction. He rolled Duncan up in the canvas sheet, then tied the shroud around him with rope. When he finished and straightened, she let the other two animals graze and ran over to help him put Duncan over her horse.

"We can ride double," he said, fastening the ropes to each stirrup to keep the body over the saddle.

She looked around as if anxious to be on their way. "You learn much in the store?"

"Frank Schade owns this place, and he won't like us taking Duncan's body to his people."

"He— I mean Duncan have a wife?"

Slocum skipped a flat rock four times over the muddy red Canadian water, until it sunk in the choppy waves. Grateful the surly-talking ferryman was across at the other side, he gave a weary shake of his head and looked at her. "I don't know. We'll have to find out."

Mounted, he leaned over with his arm in a crook and hoisted her up behind him. Red acted spooky about the deal of two aboard him, but Slocum talked him out of any foolishness and they were off leading the other two.

"Keep your heels out of his flank," he said.

"I understand," she assured him close to his ear, as she hugged his waist.

He turned down a path that followed the river and avoided reentering Schadeville, and hoped that meant no more confrontation with any of Schade's men. Through the white-barked sycamore, walnuts and patches of bamboo cane flats, he moved upstream. Be good to have this grim task over and be on their way again. They were still several days from his goal.

He could smell cooking smoke and hear children screaming in play long before they rounded a bend and could see them. When they emerged from the brush, he could make out the rail fences, crops and crude log cabins.

Children went silent. Wide brown eyes followed them. Even the dogs didn't make a sound, as if trained not to dare bark at a white man. When they reached the center of the shacks, he reined up. Several black men and women began to appear, wringing their hands.

"Anyone kin to Jim Duncan?"

A full-faced woman stepped out. "I be his aunt. My name's Sally."

Slocum nodded and let Wink down. Then he dismounted. "Jim's dead."

"We's knowed that—why you's brung him back?"

"He needs to be properly laid to rest"

"What Masa Schade say about it."

"I didn't ask him."

His words drew a titter of voices behind black hands, in concerned whispers.

"You's know he ain't gonna be happy. Not by his orders and all." Sally shook her head as if the worst could be expected.

"Is there a preacher?"

"Not one to say any words over Jim Duncan."

"Then I will," Slocum said.

The grave was hastily dug, and people began to come out of the shadows. More and more until their voices singing hymns resonated in the glen. A short man with a bible came and told Slocum he would do the services, if he didn't care.

"I don't care, but you people need to seek the law in Fort Smith. Judge Parker will defend you from the Schades in this world."

"We will, sir," an older black man said. "We have lived in fear long enough."

"See that you do." Slocum turned and started to leave. A hush fell over the crowd of sad faces. "Get the horses," he said to Wink, then turned to the crowd. "All of you are free and citizens. Stand up or the Schades in this world will always make you bow."

"Will they do what you told them?" she asked as they rode out.

He looked back. "I sure hope so."

In late evening, they rode into a small village called Delf. After looking it over, they set up camp at the edge of the town along a creek and she cooked them supper. The next morning he rode in to town to buy some coffee. Still sleepy-eyed, he blinked in disbelief at the sight he beheld. Coming across the settlement's dusty street with his limp hat brim turned down all around and unblocked, Hurricane hobbled his way.

"Some hoot owl tell you I was here?"

Hurricane looked around. "Where is she?"

"She's in camp. You must have rode by her."

"I was in Fort Smith and heard the colonel is in Dallas. So I rode down here to look for you."

"You get any word on a kid named Malloy?"

Hurricane shook his head. "No word on him or the breed."

"Reckon they still may be in this area?"

"I can help you look."

"Good, bees don't tell me much."

He looked hard at Slocum. "She won't mind if I go along?"

"No, she wants them caught."

"When we leave?"

"We can be ready in an hour."

Hurricane nodded that it suited him. "I got to see this women." He indicated up the way. "Then I will be ready."

"We'll be ready. Don't get in no trouble." Slocum grinned as Hurricane stood up stiff-like. "Your back bothering you?"

Without any expression on his bronze face, he shook his head. Then he looked around to be certain they were alone. "Last night she bucked harder than a horse."

"Be careful, she may stomp you."

Hurricane acted like he never heard him, and limped off. Slocum needed to get back and tell Wink she should be ready to go too. Whew, his back hurt too. And not from "bucking" either.

With the coffee he bought in a poke, he rode back to camp and found her busy cooking breakfast over the fire.

"Hurricane's here. Got information on the colonel. Supposed to be in Dallas."

She swept the curls back from her face. "He's here now?"

"No—he's busy right now. But he'll be ready to go in an hour or so."

She covered a yawn. "Blue here?"

"She may be home milking his cow."

"Oh."

He shrugged. "Who knows about Hurricane?"

She slipped off her perch and pulled on her boots. "He'd make a good Mormon."

Slocum chuckled. "I'm ready for some breakfast."

"It's ready."

He stepped over and hugged her. "I know it's been tough on you."

She wrapped her arms around him. "You said it would be tough, and I had to be too."

"You're doing good."

"Except yesterday."

"Huh?" He frowned at her.

"Remember those three shots I made at the tin cans yesterday? Well, I never reloaded my gun when I had the chance." She shook her head in dismay.

He squeezed her. "At least you remembered."

"Oh, I did. I got up last night and did it."

"Good girl."

She snuggled against him until he kissed her. They'd never get anywhere . . . Who gave a damn?

With Slocum full of her good food and coffee, the three-some pulled out leading the pack mule, Hurricane's red one wringing his tail and the medicine man scolding him out of bucking—though he did cow kick a few times to show off.

Slocum laughed, any moment expecting the mule to pile his old friend in a heap.

"Where we headed?" he asked him.

"Place called Curly's. He sells bad whiskey."

"Isn't it illegal to sell whiskey in the Nation?" she asked.

"Only when you get caught." Hurricane laughed and then checked his dancing mule.

"We saw Yellow Deer bring some whiskey in by paying a fine."

"She's a rich old woman too. I should marry her."

"Isn't she kinda old for your taste?" Wink teased.

"Ho, maybe I could stand her if she was real rich." Hurricane laughed until he shook.

They stopped at a crossroads store for lunch at noon. Several Indians lounged around the place and nodded to Hurricane. He and Slocum dismounted, hitching their mounts. She sat her bay and watched after them while they went inside.

The store was dark except for a few flickering candles that sent yellow light from behind shadowy goods and shelves. No one was behind the counter and they waited. Slocum wondered where the clerk might be and glanced around.

At last a middle-aged Indian woman came out. "We are closed today."

Hurricane squeezed his eyes half-shut. "Why is the door open if you are closed?"

"To let some air in. It's hot." Her glare met his.

"You have candles lit?"

"So I can see your faces when you come in, and tell you we are closed."

"Who died?"

"No one. This is my store—today I close it."

"No sign."

"Most of my customers can't read a sign."

"How do they know you are closed?"

"I tell them so."

Hurricane shook his head as Slocum pulled on his arm. "She's closed."

"I know, she told me." Hurricane turned back. "When will you be open again?"

She shrugged. "When my headache you gave me leaves."

"Dumb Choctaw," he grumbled under his breath as they went outside.

"What is wrong?" Wink asked in a stage whisper.

Slocum shook his head. "Hurricane met his match in there."

"How?"

Busy watching Hurricane shake hands with the loafers, he mounted and shook his head. "I can tell you later. The store's closed 'cause the owner has a headache he caused."

Wink chuckled. "What's he doing now?"

"Maybe organizing a protest against her." Slocum stepped into the saddle.

The bowlegged medicine man came back and nodded as he remounted. "Two miles farther down this road a white man owns a store. He is open."

When they were beyond hearing, Hurricane twisted and looked back. When he turned back, he said, "That boy called Nickel was here this morning."

"Where is he now?" Wink said, standing in the stirrups and frowning at him.

"They didn't know. Said he was looking for some guy slept with his woman."

"Nickel have a woman up here?"

"Maybe she has him—those guys laughed when that one told me someone slept with her. She must sleep with a lot of men."

"No idea what her name is?" Slocum asked.

Hurricane shook his head. "I didn't want him to know we were looking for him."

"Good. Any of the others around here?"

"I don't know. I didn't want the word out too loud." Turned in the saddle, Hurricane looked back through the post oak woods that lined the way, and then when he settled in his saddle, he shook his head. "I may give her a worse headache."

"How can we find him?" Wink asked.

"I will find where he sleeps."

"Good." She settled in her saddle and nodded as if satisfied.

"What's the plan?" Slocum asked he old man.

"We make camp at the next crossroads and you be a cattle buyer. I'll scout out where he might be."

"What'll we do with the cattle?" she asked.

"Drive them out and sell them," Slocum said. "We won't lose much money and it will make a good cover."

"May even make some money." Hurricane laughed. "Slocum can be plenty tough trading."

Barlow's Corners was in a wide, flat mountaintop meadow. The storekeeper was white and shook hands with the two when they came inside. From his neat store to his well-goomed appearance, Slocum considered Silver Barlow a sharp businessman. In his thirties, he had two breed sons in their teens and an Indian wife, Mona, who greeted Wink—and they had lots to talk about.

"You can pasture the cattle you buy for ten cents a week. The boys will herd them."

"Six bits a day be enough pay?" Slocum asked the oldest one, called Arrow.

He smiled. "How many drovers you need?"

Slocum laughed and held up two fingers.

"We will be ready when you are, sir. Thank you." Arrow said, and the boys went off.

Mona fed them rich beef stew and homemade sourdough bread for lunch. After the meal, Slocum bought some canvas and rope. Barlow told them where they could set up camp close by and also use a corral for their horses and mules. The two of them made a shade and fly with the canvas and rope, using trees and some poles. Then they cut back the brush until they had a camp.

When Slocum looked up from his finished ax job and stretched his back muscles, the setting sun's red glare was in his eyes. The smell of Wink's cooking filled his nose, along with the pungent oak-smelling cooking fire.

"Where's Hurricane?" he asked, dropping on a wood block seat.

Bent over her Dutch oven, she looked up at him. "He went to see about her headache, he said."

Slocum yawned. "Okay, what's for supper?"

"Biscuits. I borrowed some starter. Making enough for breakfast too. Some beef, some potatoes and fresh green beans Mona gave me."

"I'm ready." He laughed and rose stiff. "I better wash up."

She brought a kettle of hot water and carried it over to

put some in the wash pan. "You think he'll learn where Nickel is?"

"Anyone can learn something from these people, he can."

"Good." She stared across the yellow brown meadow that stretched far to the west and up the side of the far mountain.

"It won't be easy," he said and threw his arms around her. "Obviously, the gang's split up." Hugged tight to her, he nuzzled her neck under the curls.

"Guess that means we have time to play?"

"After supper," he said and cupped her breasts under the shirt.

"Ah, you are weak from all the work."

"No, but right now, I'm starved."

"All right, just so you aren't giving other women headaches, I'll feed you."

Slocum laughed and hung his arm over her shoulder going back to the campfire.

8

The old man must have learned something—he wanted to move on, the cattle deal was off and they were headed south. They rolled up the canvas and packed the mule before sunup and were started out on what Hurricane called the Texas Road. Slocum knew any road headed south was called that, as they were in reverse called the Kansas Road, which did not mean more than that a traveler who kept going would get to those places. The hills became higher and the country rougher as the day wore on for the three of them.

The streams were rock-lined and the water flowed over them clear. They passed several homesteads with cooking smoke and small plots of sun-dried corn stalks—some of them already bundled in shocks. Naked brown children peered at them and black cur dogs barked at a safe distance. Sometimes women looked in their direction from hanging wash; others stopped to peer tossing out wastewater from the door frames of their log homes.

Several wagons clattered along with a hard-eyed Indian man holding the lines. He looked them over while his woman, beside him, applied a whip to the thin mismatched horses jogging stiffly with a jingle of harness. They met and passed several others, and were forced to get over so the wheeled carriages could use the ruts cut between the seed-headed grass. Slocum always nodded or touched his hat brim, and never expected a gesture in return from the stone-faced men. Hurricane acted like the others were invisible.

"Guess you don't know any of them we passed," Slocum said, looking back as the last rattling rig went north.

"They are Choctaws mostly. Why should I speak to them? You speak to every dog you see?"

"No."

Wink chuckled and shook her head, riding on the far side of Slocum. "But they're your people."

"Not mine, mine are Cherokee."

"But I thought all Indians were brothers?"

He frowned at her. "Who said that?"

"I'm not sure—may have been a white man."

Hurricane nodded as if satisfied she knew her own answer.

"We can stop for lunch at the next flat place with some feed for the animals," Slocum said.

Hurricane and Wink agreed.

She fed them dry cheese, crackers and some pepper jerky. Seated on the ground under an ancient oak, serenaded by crows, they washed down lunch in the strong south wind that swept some of the midday heat away.

"We can stop at Jetter's Store tonight," Hurricane said.

"When will we get there?" she asked, seated beside Slocum in the grass.

"After dark."

"How much farther?" she asked.

"Maybe twenty miles."

"Is that the area where you think some of them might be?" Slocum asked.

"Malloy may be around there or farther down."

Slocum nodded and she did too.

The moon wasn't up, and the stars gave little light after twilight. Hurricane led the way, and they hurried as fast as they dared. Slocum was beginning to wish they'd simply

stopped earlier and set up camp, but Hurricane acted determined to get there.

When they finally dismounted at the hitch rack, dim
lights glowed in the small windows of the store building.

"Ho, Jetter," Hurricane shouted, before they stepped on
the porch.

"Down!" he shouted at the metallic click of a gun. A barrage of red-flamed gunshots came from the store's open doorway. With her still in the saddle, Wink's bay went to bucking.
Slocum fired one shot at the doorway. Then realizing the dan-
ger to her, he ran after her shouting, "Get off! Get off him."

She hit the ground facedown and he was beside her.
"Keep down. You all right?"

"I . . . I'm fine. What happened?"

Beside her on his knees, with a pistol in his hand, he tried
to appraise the situation. "We rode into a trap."

Sounds of horses and confusion behind the store
reached him.

"Stay here." Slocum was on his feet; his purpose was to
get a shot at them. He rushed around the building and emptied his six-gun after the shadowy figures fast disappearing
into the night's arms.

"She okay?" Hurricane asked, joining him.

"Says she is." Slocum reloaded his Colt with bullets from
his gunbelt.

"Good. Better see about Jetter."

"Was that our welcome?" Slocum asked him as she
joined them and he hugged her shoulder. "Too damn close."
He slapped the six-gun back in his holster.

"Real close," she said with a shudder and they followed
Hurricane inside.

"Those sumbitches knew too much about our business,"
Hurricane grumbled in the room's darkness. "Some gawdamn Choctaw must have told them we were coming here."

Feet stomping on the floor made them both draw their
guns. Hurricane lighted a coal oil lamp, and Slocum saw a

gray-headed man and a younger Indian woman bound and gagged behind the counter.

"Who did this?" Slocum asked, ungagging and then untying the woman.

"They were three of them," she managed, trying to get her breath as Hurricane freed the man.

"That damn Nickel Malloy was the leader. Peter Twohorse and that Lanny boy were with him; they came in and jumped us. Said they were going to kill some guys who were after them," Jetter said as Wink led the missus aside into a shed attached to the building.

"He's been acting the big shot around here for several days. Trying to get some more to join his gang." Jetter, a thin man in his fifties, looked around to be sure they were alone before he spoke again. "I'd sent word to the U.S. marshal at Fort Smith a few days ago about him and his activities."

He dropped his elbows on the counter and shook his head as if to clear it. Then he shouted at the side room. "Betty, you all right?"

"I'm fine, Ira," she said, sweeping her black hair back from her face and peering at them from the doorway. "Your woman and I are going to fix some food. She said you had not eaten yet either."

Slocum thanked her and she returned to the living quarters.

"Where's he buying his whiskey?" Hurricane asked, wrinkling his nose. "It's stronger than the gunpowder smell in here."

"Maybe at Fred's Ranch." Jetter turned his palms up.

Hurricane nodded as if he knew the place. "Fred keeps some ugly whores and sells bad whiskey there."

"We better check that out come daylight. I'm going to go find our horses," Slocum said.

"Need a lamp?" Jetter offered.

"I'll know more later. Moon's coming up. Better go see if I can even find them."

"I'm coming too," Hurricane said and joined him.

The sorrel and two mules were grazing less than fifty yards away from the store. Hurricane took the two mules back to unload. Slocum tightened the cinch and threw his leg over Red.

"I'll go look for her horse."

"Be careful—they might sneak back."

"I will." He reined Red around. No telling how far the bay had gone. He rode out the tracks going north in the last direction he'd seen the horse take after tossing her. Sticking to the moonlit road, he hoped that the bay, having been with the sorrel so long, would nicker or give a sound to him out of the dark shadowy post oaks. But nothing showed up after the first two miles, so he decided to wait until daylight.

When he loped up, Wink rushed out to check on him. "You all right?"

"Yes, but no horse." He dismounted and she hugged him. "We'll find him after daylight."

"Better wash up and come eat," she said to him.

"Fine." Hungry enough to eat a bear, he wondered about Nickel and his plans in the future. Obviously their identity was blown. How had they known Slocum was coming after them?

She hugged his arm. "I was sure scared when the shooting started."

"What did I tell you, this is a damn tough business."

You're right." She released him so he could wash up on the porch. "But next time, I'll be more ready—I know what I did wrong."

"What's that?" he asked.

"I forgot the pale face of my son when I first saw him that day."

He shook his head and put down the towel. "More to it than that."

She shook her head and then swept the curls back as they entered the store. "You'll see."

* * *

Dawn came in a humid mist. Slocum found the bay, saddle and all, standing grazing with the others when he went out to check on them. He caught him and slipped a rope around his neck—the reins were broken, but he looked sound and the saddle fine. The bay hobbled just in case, Slocum took the headstall back with him to the store for new reins.

"Bay's back," he said, meeting her on the porch.

"Good. I was worried he might have really run away."

"All you worried about was you'd have to ride a mule."

She laughed and shook her head at his teasing. "Yes, that too."

After breakfast, he had completed the bridle repairs and the threesome was ready to ride to Fred's. Their camping things tucked under the tarp for their return and the pack mule hobbled so he wouldn't follow them, they rode out with Jetter's warning to expect some tough ones to be there. The lonesome braying of the left-behind mule trailed them.

They rode over a pass, mid-morning, the day's heat rising. A free wind swept Slocum's face as they paused to let their horses get their breath. He took Wink's reins as she dismounted and excused herself to seek some relief in the privacy of the brush.

"We close to the ranch?" he asked Hurricane.

The old man nodded. "It's in this valley."

"Good. You think they're there?"

His dark eyes narrowed to slits as he studied the land beneath them. "Who knows where such wolves will rest at."

"I guess you're right. Vast country."

"We will know soon."

"Good." He handed Wink the reins. "We're close to the place."

"Good." She remounted, and they set off down the trail.

Slocum checked the loads in his Colt and reholstered it, satisfied it was all right. He turned and nodded to Wink, then paused to see the hard set in her face. The night before's experience had obviously not turned aside her determination—so she was tough enough for whatever lay ahead.

They came through some cut-off timber, and Hurricane pointed to the east. Slocum could see a cedar-shingle roof and nodded. "That it?"

"He usually has a lookout on the roof."

"We better go on foot from here."

Hurricane agreed and they dismounted. Horses hobbled, they moved to the north, the shorter man in the lead and Slocum behind Wink, all three of them on edge as they hurried through the brush and a few spindly trees spared the ax. In minutes, they squatted on the border of the clearing and studied the corrals and back of the new log house.

"No guard on roof," Hurricane said under his breath.

Slocum nodded. "We need to run off the horses. Then they can't escape if they're here."

"I can do that," she said.

Hurricane looked at her. "You may have to shoot one of them."

Her eyes narrowed. "I can do that too."

"Don't close your eyes," Slocum said and put his hand on her shoulders. "When you turn the horses loose, they'll descend on you."

She nodded.

"Turn the horses out and then get on the far side of the corral." Slocum felt uncertain about the decision, but certain he couldn't protect her forever in her determination to get the killers. "We're going to try and stop them."

"Let's go," Hurricane said, his double barrel at the ready.

Slocum nodded to her and headed after the Cherokee. They went past the chimney and headed for the porch on the front. When he looked back, she had already gone to release the horses. Pistol in his fist, he followed Hurricane around the building, and a man seated in a rocking chair jumped up. The rifle across his lap clattered to the floor.

"Who the hell—"

Hurricane's tough look and the poke of the shotgun muzzle cut off his protest as his face paled.

"Who's in there?" Hurricane demanded.

"No one—"

Hurricane jammed the gun barrels in his gut to enforce his question.

"Nickel, Fred, Two-hoss—"

A quick nod to Slocum, and Hurricane shoved the man down in the chair. "Don't move."

"I-I won't." The man trembled in fear, grasping the arms of the rocker.

A gray-haired man rushed out on the porch. "What the hell's going on with the horses—"

The man's color drained from his face at the sight of the shotgun. He put his hands out as if to ward it off. "Who the fuck are you?"

"The one came to kill you."

"God, no."

"Tell them we have them surrounded—come out or we'll burn them up."

Slocum positioned himself beside the door. The first figure came out gun cocked. Slocum busted him so hard on the shoulder with his Colt, the outlaw fired his revolver into the floorboards. He went to his knees screaming in pain. Slocum wrenched the gun out of his hand and threw it way. With his boot, he shoved the crying man aside and faced the open door, his pistol cocked.

Hearing shots in the back, he dove into the room and could see that the back door was open. He swore and tried to focus in the darkness. A pistol's orange blast from the side of the room made him duck, emptying his own revolver in that direction. Acrid smoke boiled up in the room; he dared not move from the gritty floor. He could hear some spurs kicking the floor—no doubt in death throes.

He lay on his belly, feeding fresh rounds into the Colt and listening.

"Slocum?" It was Hurricane at the front door.

"I'm fine. I don't think he is." Colt loaded at last, he rose slow to his knees and looked at the open back doorway. Where was she? "You okay, Wink?"

"I think so," she said in a small voice outside.

"You hit?" he asked.

"No. But he is."

"Who?"

"Not Nickel."

"I think he's in here." He struck a match and lit a candle lamp. Carrying it, he went to where the pimple-faced kid was sprawled on his back. His blue eyes stared at the split-shingle ceiling—he wouldn't shoot any more innocent boys. Slocum holstered his gun and went to the back door.

Seated on the ground, .32 in her lap, she looked up at him with wet eyelashes. On the ground, facedown, was the body of a man with a pistol in his outstretched hand.

"He came out to kill me."

Slocum nodded, went over and sat down beside her. He draped an arm over her shoulder. "I know that. This ain't an easy business."

She holstered the pistol and rose into his arms, burying her face in his shoulder. "I'm learning. I'm learning."

"Nickel's dead." He rocked her in his hug and then raised her face to look at him.

"That doesn't even matter at the moment. I wanted to celebrate every one of them being sent to hell—it isn't like that, is it?"

Stabbed by her words, he held her tight and closed his eyes. "No, it never is."

She blinked her wet lashes at him. "I still want the rest of them."

"I understand."

9

They left Fred's Ranch after Fred and his man Carl buried Peter Two-horse and Nickel Malloy. Fred told them that the third member of Nickel's gang, Amos Lanny, had quit the bunch and ran off the night before. The fact satisfied them, and they rode back to Jetter's, arriving there at sundown.

A tall man in a suit and a narrow-brim felt hat was introduced to them before Jetter's wife Betty ran off to fix more food. Wink fell in to help her after learning the man's name: Deputy U.S. Marshal Fred Burns, from Fort Smith.

"So Nickel is dead?" he asked after shaking their hands.

Slocum nodded. "So is Peter Two-horse."

"The Indian Territory is two better off," he said. "I won't fill that out in my report, but I'm grateful."

"There is an Indian called Indian Tee who was with the criminals that murdered her son and husband in Kansas," Slocum said.

"Willy Tee—likes to be called Black Hawk."

"I don't know—but he was with Nickel, Colonel Bowdry, the leader, and Henny Williams at the murder–robbery."

"Willy Tee has some folks up by Choteau on the Grand

River. We have some warrants for him. He's a mean sumbitch, and they will hide him."

"All these guys are, and Bowdry is no exception."

Burns nodded. "Him and his gang robbed a mail car last spring. There's a five hundred dollar reward on him."

"I think he may be back in Texas," Slocum said.

"Could be," Burns agreed.

"Henny Williams?" Hurricane asked.

"That's the skinny cowboy that murders women." Burns shook his head with a wary set to his lips. "He can slip through a knothole. We had him cornered up on the Canadian and he got away. Two marshals captured him near Fenton, and at night he slipped his cuffs and got away."

"I guess we'll go look for them," Slocum said when Wink called them to come and eat.

"Don't envy you. Guess we owe you for stopping that damn Nickel from forming another gang and going on a rampage up here."

"No problem."

After the meal, Slocum shook hands with Burns, excused himself and joined Wink at their things. He took up their bedrolls and laughed looking at the stars. "No rain tonight. Guess we don't need a tent."

She hooked her hand in his elbow, and they followed a silver path through the trees, to an open spot of grazed down grass. He unfurled the first bed and she caught his arm. "We only need one."

He smiled and toed off a boot, watching her undo the buttons on her shirt in the pearl light. She glanced up in the shadowy light and smiled as if embarrassed. "No modesty left in me, is there?"

Out of a strong impulse, he swept her into his arms and kissed her. "Been a tough day. I'm here to make you forget it."

Her palms framed his face and she pulled him back. "Yes," escaped her lips before they closed on his.

Clothes melted away like peeling a fruit, until they soon stood naked in each other's arms. They scrambled to lie on the bedroll, her knees raised and parted for him and her arms held open. Firm breasts soon poked his chest, and his hips ached to hunch into her in those moments before connection, when the urges of both for the attachment rose to a crescendo. Her hand shot down for the turgid shaft and directed the swollen head to her moist lips. He slid in with the power of a pile driver, and a new electricity struck his brain like lightning. The strong ring of fire closed on him like a vise, and she cried out in passion's arms. Her legs widened to admit him deeper and he hunched hard for that position.

Leaning forward on his braced arms, he began to feel her clit scratch the surface of his probe. His thrusts grew faster and her contractions tighter and tighter, until he and she were raging for their breath in a whirlwind of maddened pumping.

She raised her hips for all of him. The skintight head of his dick ached. More and more, faster and faster, harder and harder, until he felt the fire rise in the depth of his balls. He moved as deep as he could go and she clutched him. The explosion fountained out of him like a hard shot, draining his strength and letting all things pass.

"Oh, God," she moaned and threw her arms out in surrender. "Oh, I'm sorry to keep talking about the poor man—but if Walter could see me now—he'd die. I can recall him fumbling around like it was something I must endure." She closed her eyes and shook her head. "I'm such a slut—such a slut."

"Why?" he asked, slipping beside her silky body.

"I like it. I love it. I could do it all the time."

"Hey, it's for you to enjoy."

"I'll remember that. To enjoy." She snuggled against him. "What next?"

"Sleep some."

"I think I can now." She raised up and kissed him. "Billy Bob never lied to me about hiring you. He said you were the man—I didn't know then what he meant."

He hugged her and smiled.

* * *

"Where are we headed?" she asked him, pushing the bay up close beside him. In the shadowy first light, soft purple doves, feeding on the ripe grass seed, burst into the air at their approach and caused her horse to spook some. But she held him in check and forced him back in place.

"Guess all the information comes out of Fort Smith. I figured we'd go up there and check around. Bound to be a rumor about the others. Besides, it's on the way to Choteau."

"Indian Tee," she said, as if rolling the name over, and nodded slow in approval.

"Or who else he calls himself."

"Black Hawk," she added

"He won't be easy to catch," Hurricane said. "He can be like a ghost."

She turned in the saddle and frowned at him bringing up the rear leading the pack mule. "There ain't real ghosts."

"Don't bet money," Hurricane said. "He can become one."

"No way. What do you think, Slocum?"

"I think ol' Doc Hurricane says he's a ghost, I wouldn't bet against him." He twisted in the saddle to look at the stone-faced Cherokee and then turned back.

"I don't believe it," she said.

"Guess we'll see," Slocum said.

After camping one night at the base of the mountains and a dusty hot ride by late afternoon, they rode the ferry across the Arkansas and could see sunset shining on the brick buildings of downtown Fort Smith.

"Is it dangerous for you to be here?" she whispered over the paddle wheel thrashing the water on the side of the barge.

"No more than anywhere else," he said, holding the bridle reins of the two horses so they didn't spook.

She rubbed her hands on the front of her pants. "I guess I need a dress."

"We can get one. How about a real bath?"

"Maybe two to get the grit and the horse off me." She smiled at the prospect. "Why did Hurricane insist on staying over there in that shack town across the river?"

"Probably knew some woman." Slocum laughed.

She shook her head as if embarrassed and then laughed. "Plenty of smoke in his old chimney too."

They left their horses at Bell's Livery and walked through the crowd with the barkers extolling the virtues of the saloons and eateries on Garrison Avenue. A few policemen strode the walks, along with drovers in Texas gear, river men who'd no doubt brought or come in on the paddle boats docked near the ferry crossing. Indians stood with their backs to the wall staring at nothing; squaws sat on the ground beside them. Some high-priced whores in their low-cut silk dresses, under parasols despite the twilight's fleeting cast, walked like queens toward their places, perhaps to stand behind some big-betting gambler, or to lounge in a rich man's suite, a man who could afford their outrageous fees.

He guided her into a millinery shop. A woman came from the back and smiled looking her all over, and then frowned at her attire.

"Good evening."

"Good evening. Do you have anything ready made I might fit in?" Wink asked, looking around at the various dresses.

"Oh, yes, Miss . . ."

"Mrs. White," Wink corrected her.

"I am so sorry."

"That's all right. Fashion is not my interest. I need a dress."

The woman frowned. "You don't want a bustle?"

She looked at Slocum, who stood back, then shook her head—no bustle. He shrugged.

"You know the fashion is—"

"I know. I want a dress I can simply wear in town."

"I have a blue dress in back that might fit you with some

work. Unfortunately the lady we made it for had to leave town, so I could sell it to you at a discount."

They waited. The woman soon returned and spread the deep blue dress out for Wink's inspection. It buttoned to the throat, and the skirt portion was billowy.

Wink looked to Slocum, who nodded.

"I'll try it on."

"You may go in the back. I'll show you," the woman said.

"I'll also need some unmentionables," Wink said as they started for the curtained doorway.

"Oh, yes, I have them."

Wink came back from the rear, and he nodded his approval at first sight. The dress fit well, and she looked very feminine carrying the hem. She spun around and laughed. "Walter would die if he was here. Me paying thirty dollars for a dress."

"So? It looks good."

"She is going to hem it high enough it won't drag wearing my boots under it."

"Good idea."

Her mouth full of straight pins, the woman knelt and began testing the hem length. The distance set and pinned, she rose. "It will be ready in two hours, Mrs. White."

"You stay open that late?" Wink asked.

"Oh, yes, especially for a customer."

"Better change," he said. "So she can get started."

"I shall." Wink swept away with the seamstress on her heels.

They left the millinery and headed up Garrison. The cowboy hat resting on her shoulders, she drew some looks in the dim light filtering out of stores and joints along the board sidewalk. Slocum heard "Texas gal" from several onlookers. He directed her into Phillip's Chop House and the maître d' frowned. Slocum shook his head. "A private booth for the Missus and me?"

"Of course, sir." And he showed them to one that was turned so no one except the service people could observe them.

"I thought at first he would turn us away," she said, sliding in opposite him.

Slocum shook his head. "Hell, there's probably a half dozen rich businessmen in here with their concubines."

"Concubine—my, I never thought about that word." Then she put her hands over her mouth to laugh.

"Wine, sir?" The waiter offered a bottle.

"Ever had any good wine?" he asked her.

"Had some elderberry once when I was little girl in Iowa."

"Ah, bring us a bottle of some French wine. We're celebrating."

"*Oui, monsieur.*"

"What are we celebrating?" she hissed.

"Ah, Malloy is off the slate and you're getting a bath soon and a new dress."

"And we'll sleep tonight in a bed." Then she winked mischievously at him. "I bet it won't be any better than the ground."

"Who knows?" He chuckled and reached over to squeeze both of her hands. Then he closed his eyes and thought about his dog days in the war, drinking out of cow tracks, eating wild mushrooms raw and grateful for them, maggots in the bacon they doled out to them and cooking it on sticks over an open fire, fields of the silent dead, the uncountable amputees, the hollow-eyed citizens raped and plundered, then burned out, who were lined along the roads. They looked like corpses standing there, no food and no hope.

At last the waiter brought the wine and the fine crystal glasses. He poured a sample, swirled it and handed it to Slocum to taste.

After the sip, he nodded his approval and the man filled their glasses and left. The wine mellowed them, so when their large platters of food came they both were laughing.

"What is all this?" she asked, looking over it in amazement.

"Eat," he said and grinned. "I didn't order the full portion.'

"Oh, my. I couldn't eat all this in two days."

"Fun to try," he said and cut into the thick steak—tender, and in his mouth the richness drew the saliva in a flood. "Best place to eat on the border."

"Expensive dress, expensive meal—oh my, how will I ever go back to beans?"

"You still have money?"

"Oh, yes. Why, will you need some?"

He shook his head. "I don't want you to spend all of it."

"I owe you—"

"Not yet, but we need to put some of that money in a safe deposit box."

"Good idea. I had no idea, and the way banks have failed—" She looked hard at him for her answer.

He poured her some more wine. "If they can't get their hands on it, it'll be all right."

"Fine. We can do that here?"

"In the morning, whenever we get up."

"Whenever," she said, looking dreamily at him. "Oh, my, this food is so good."

"Whenever," he said, cutting another bit off the browned steak.

10

Early the next morning, Slocum found Izzac Brower seated at a table in the Chinese café called Chow-Chow's, in the basement of the Seaman's building. Red-eyed and looking hungover, the man, in his forties, barely glanced up when Slocum entered the café, and only at last nodded for Slocum to join him.

Slocum crossed the room that smelled of ginger and spices and took out a chair to sit on. The Asian waiter came over and bowed. "You want food?"

"Just black coffee."

"Good. Me get you some."

"Thanks."

"I heard you were in town, Slocum," Brower said, over the steaming crock mug he held in both hands.

"You get lots of news."

"Some I do, some I don't."

"Indian Tee?"

Brower looked around as if to appraise the entire room, half-filled with the same sort of crowd on the street the night before, without any blacks or Indians. Finally Brower spoke. "He's a mean sumbitch. Ain't been a marshal able to arrest

him yet. I bet he's killed two of them at the least, but proving
he done it might be hard."

"Then they want him?"

He wrinkled his nose. "Not that bad."

"What's he do—thanks," he said to the waiter who delivered his coffee.

"He has lots of kin up there to hide him. Plus he scares
the rest. Give you a good example."

Slocum looked up, wondering why he had stopped.

Brower nodded and began again. "He went over to this
guy's house one night who lives up there, told him to make
his wife take off all her clothes and get on the bed. Then he
screwed her while he made the guy watch him do it."

"Did the husband do anything?"

Bower shook his head. "He's done it several times."

"Same guy?"

"Yeah, and others."

"Why don't someone kill him?" Slocum blew on the
steam and considered sipping his coffee.

"Afraid—very afraid."

"Would any of them help me?"

"I don't think so—too afraid."

"Anyone that mean around here for hire?"

"No."

"Brower, you know them all. Surely there is one who for
a price would go up there and help me."

"I'll check. Where are you staying?"

"Grand Hotel."

Brower made a face that he approved. "Traveling good
this time."

"The queen of hearts has been kind to me, let's say."

"But why Tee?" Brower shook his head in disapproval.
"Why the fuck do you want him anyway?"

"He was with a gang that killed a man and a boy in
Kansas in a robbery and shooting spree."

"I see. I'll look for someone, but promise nothing."

"Good. I have to get back." He laid a twenty-dollar gold piece on the table before the man.

Brower nodded in approval at the deposit. "See ya. I got the coffee."

Word came an hour later to the hotel. Slocum studied the message and nodded to himself.

"Bad news?" she asked, seated on the bed, brushing her hair.

"No, but I need to go meet a man." Excusing himself, he left the room. The gunman Brower had found for him was to be waiting at a back table in Clauncy's Saloon on Garrison.

"Barkeep said your name was Smith." Slocum stood over the man, who slouched his paunchy frame in a captain's chair. Full-faced, his green eyes had never left Slocum since he'd entered the deserted place.

"I'm Smith," he drawled out the left side of his mouth, like he only used that half to speak. "You must be Slocum." He motioned to another chair. "Whatcha got on your mind?"

"An Indian named Tee up around Choteau."

"Dead or alive?"

"I don't care."

"You tailing along?"

"I can, or I can meet you there if you decide you need help."

"I usually work alone. Like it that way; then I don't got anyone to worry about. I'll bring you his head for a hundred dollars—proof enough?" He fingered a large elk tooth on a gold chain that hung on his vest.

"Proof enough. How much time you need?"

"There's a depot up there. I'll meet you there at noon Friday if I get him."

"His corpse might get you a reward too."

"Fine. What's that worth?"

"I'll check with the U.S. marshal."

Smith nodded. "Friday at the train depot. Have the cash."

Leaned back, Slocum nodded and shook his head at the bartender's offer to get him a drink. "I'm leaving."

Smith reached out and tugged on his shirtsleeve. "Brower says you'll pay me; otherwise I'd want the money up front."

"I'll have it in cash."

A nod, and Smith rose, stretched, knifed in his shirttail with his flat hand and went out the swinging doors. By the time Slocum reached the sidewalk, he was gone. Brower knew the tough ones—Smith, or whatever his name was, fit the mold. Slocum went back to the hotel room.

"How did it go?" she asked.

"He says to meet him Friday at the depot up there. He asked for a hundred dollars."

"Think he can do it?"

Slocum went to the window and looked down on the traffic. "He's a man about thirty-five, who lives by his wits. I think he'll be there."

"A hundred cash. That the going rate?"

He turned back and shrugged. "I guess. This Tee is a tough guy. He gets by with lots of lawlessness up there."

She came over and hugged his arm. "What will we do?"

He used his finger to turn her chin up and kissed her. Then he pushed the robe off her shoulders and exposed her naked body. His hand sought her right breast and gently squeezed it. "I think we can occupy our spare time in the meanwhile."

Friday, they rode into Choteau. Hurricane had gone home to check on Blue, so the two of them came up the road parallel to the Katy Tracks from Fort Gibson. The red train station loomed ahead, and a few scattered houses on the grassy prairie and some false-front stores huddled in a row made up the town.

Some dark object sat atop a post at the end of the train platform. Slocum squinted at it in the distance. Unable to figure it out, he told Wink to stay there and loped ahead. When he drew close, he saw the reddish hair fluff in the wind. The mouth open like he spoke from it, his green eyes open too, it made a gruesome sight. Smith's severed head was nailed on top of the post.

Aghast, she screamed when she rode up before he could stop her. Pale-faced, she turned away. "Who is it?"

"Our man Smith."

"How did Tee know?"

"Probably tortured him until he had all the information." He dismounted and tied Red at the rail. "I'll check inside."

The man under the green celluloid visor at the telegraph key nodded. "Was he expecting you?"

Slocum never replied to his question. "How long has he been out there?"

"Must have put him up there last night. First I saw him was this morning when I got here. I wired the marshal in Fort Smith. He's sending a deputy. You know him, mister?"

"Night man know anything?"

The operator shook his head to dismiss his question. "I never seen him before; he ain't from around here. Who is he?"

Slocum thanked him and answered the man's request for the post resident's name with "I'm not sure."

"What now?" she asked, looking around warily as they stood at the hitch rack and talked in low voices.

No rigs at any of the stores, no one out in sight, not even children—no clothes even drying on lines. No dogs barked—all that made Slocum wonder.

"I guess I need to find him. Maybe you should go up to Hurricane's place and stay till it's over."

She chewed on a knuckle and looked in deep despair over the situation. "Hurricane—he mentioned a ghost."

"Indians believe in them. But they usually are flesh and blood."

"Smith must have told him about us."

"No, Smith only knew about me. I never mentioned you."

"The robbery—murder?" She hugged her arms as the wind picked up and tousled her curls. The hat on her back, her worried face looked so fresh in the midday sunshine. Why couldn't they be back at the hotel room making love? Her sleek skin pressed against him, wanton desire, the fiery blinding passion, the endless hunger of his mouth to kiss, suck, to tease her for more and more. The ache in his butt to drive inside her deeper for more and more. In the windswept street, with tiny puffs of dust blowing off the surface, all that seemed so far away, farther than Fort Smith.

"We don't have our camping gear," he said. "He must know why we came. We better both head for Hurricane's and regroup."

"You think he's out there—watching us."

"He has eyes, he is."

"Kind of eerie, isn't it?"

He nodded. Damn eerie. After another check around, he helped her into the saddle. Then he stepped into his own stirrup and threw his leg over the cantle. He looked around the deserted country. Where was everyone? Hiding in fear of Tee? Be good to be out of this country. He gave her a head toss and booted Red up the road. Smith had been no fool— this one might be the toughest one of the bunch.

That evening Hurricane came out on the porch and smiled at the sight of Wink. Dismounted, she pecked him on the cheek and went in. She and Blue hugged in the doorway then, talking a hundred words a minute, went inside to fix some food. Hurricane came to where Slocum was uncinching the horses in the dying twilight.

"Did you get him?"

Slocum shook his head. "I hired a tough gunhand in Fort Smith. He was to meet me in Choteau at noon today."

"He meet you?"

"His head nailed on a fence post did."

"Must be tough."

"The guy called himself Smith was tough. He'd been around."

"What now?"

"You got any ideas?"

"Maybe get Arkansas Tom and Jim Lowe to go with us. Plenty mean guys."

"This Tee is a mean SOB. He runs that town and country around there. Can we get them, those two you named?"

"We can find them, we can."

"Good. Let's go find them in the morning. I have an itch in my neck. He may have tortured all the information about me from Smith, since he tacked the head up at the station for me to see on the day I'd told Smith I'd meet him there."

"We go find them," Hurricane agreed. "I think she gets prettier every time I see her."

"Wink?"

"Sure, who else rides with you?" He laughed and clapped him on the shoulder. "Maybe you should settle down with her. Sleeping alone on the ground can make you stiff and old before your time."

"Wish I could—they'd come; they always do." He cast a look around the dark grounds that surrounded the lighted cabin, then nodded and went inside.

The rich smell of Blue's cooking filled the air. A breeze gently swayed the curtains, and he took a chair that Hurricane offered him, with his back to the wall. Gut feelings made him on edge—he followed them. This one about Indian Tee was knifing him more than the usual things he fretted over. Better not let down his guard.

The beef stew Blue served them was piping hot and rich. The conversation over the meal was mostly about Fort Smith. Her fresh sourdough bread and butter added to the delight of her food, and Slocum buttered several pieces. They wouldn't sleep in the shed—he better be more careful for Wink's sake.

At bedtime, they left the house, and, walking to the shed, he whispered, "We'll get our bedrolls he left in there for us and sleep outside."

"What's wrong?"

"I'm not sure. Just uneasy about the whole deal. Just a precaution."

"You think he followed us up here?" she whispered, looking around.

Slocum searched in the inky night. "It won't hurt to be on guard."

"We need to take turns being on guard?"

"I'll take the first shift."

"Wake me up when you need to sleep."

"I will. Keep your gun ready. We may need it."

At last, their rolls spread under the low boughs of a cedar tree, and the pungent pitchy smell in his nose, he could see the shed well in the starlight. Anyone came looking for them, he'd have a good chance to make them out.

The night insects sizzled in the trees, and a horse or mule snorted in the pen. Bats swooped by catching their nocturnal meals. A distant cow bawled for a separated calf. A distant hound bayed in the star-flecked night. Hours passed. Slocum let her sleep in peace close by. The vision of Smith's head nailed on the post was lesson enough for him; this Tee was no simple renegade, and tough as any he'd ever had to face.

Something moved near the house. Only a shadow, he thought, but he'd seen it only for a glimpse. He eased out from under the tree and crouched low, moved to the shed. Gun in his sweaty right hand, he tried to peer in the darkness for another move. Sweat ran into his eyes and stung them— nothing. Had he imagined it?

This became a waiting game. Was the attacker checking the house for them? Could he be? Slocum's heart beat loud enough to deafen him. His next move had to be to get into the open. Then he saw a foot and a leg as someone slipped into the starlighted side of the cabin. Hatless, he eased himself toward the side window, which would put him near Hurricane and Blue's bed.

"Hold it there!" Slocum shouted.

The man whirled and fired a pistol point-blank at him. The orange blast from the gun muzzle flared in the night. Slocum answered with his own and knew the man was hit, but he ran off into the darkness toward the pens before Slocum could shoot him again.

"What happened?" Hurricane shouted.

"We've got company. He's hit and he ran for the barn." Slocum kept low, looking very hard for any sign.

"I'll come from this side," Hurricane said, and the sound of his shotgun being locked was loud outside where Slocum crouched beside a small coop.

The horses snorted and stomped around as if woken up. A gate creaked, and someone low on a horse screamed at the others to leave and be part of his cover. They raced by Slocum and separated, but the rider was gone into the night on one of them.

"Where's he hit?" Hurricane asked, joining him.

"I'm not sure." Slocum looked around the side of the cabin and came up with a pistol. "Maybe in the arm. Here's his gun."

"You all right?" Wink asked from the side of the shed.

"No one here's hurt. He's gone." Slocum looked off in the inkiness and saw nothing but the outline of hills and trees.

She rushed over and hugged his arm. "He's the one killed Smith, isn't he?"

"I didn't see him close enough. But I'm sure it was him."

"Sumbitch." Hurricane swore under his breath. "I hate a damn horse thief."

"We can't do anything tonight. We'll round them up in the morning," Slocum said.

"Maybe he'll bleed to death," Hurricane said in disgust. "Some of them will come back by then."

"Good night," Slocum said, punching an empty out and reloading his Colt. He spun the chamber around, holstered the gun and put his arm over Wink's shoulder.

"You never woke me."

"I was saving that for better things,"

She looked up and laughed. "I bet you were."

In a few minutes they were in the bed, naked and bodies intertwined. His hips pushed his erection in and out of her while she shoved her rock-hard nipples on stems into his chest.

"Oh, how could something so horrible turn out to be sooo nice," she moaned, and raised her hips for him to go deeper.

"Soooo nice," he repeated, and went faster.

Dawn came on a cool wind. Slocum stood in the door, listened to the rooster's crowing and studied the gray outlines of the loose horses and mules who had returned and were grazing across the flat. It was too peaceful. The animals were too close together, like they'd been herded back to there—not loose like stragglers. He recalled his buffalo hunter days; Indians under wolf skins could creep close enough to the herd to make a shot with their smaller rifles because wolves were always at the outskirts of the herd.

In the doorway, he squatted and waited. In the next few minutes, the light would increase perhaps enough to expose anyone concealed on the ground. He saw movement behind a bush. It could have been a wren flitting on the branches. But he doubted it. With his right hand, he eased out the six-gun and cocked the hammer close to his side. A rifle would be the weapon of choice at this distance—but no time to get one.

Slocum stared hard and waited. Time clicked by and nothing happened. The temperature began to replace the night's coolness. Light flooded the meadow, and the horses lifted their heads to look to the east. Tee must be leaving.

Slocum set out in a trot. The animals parted and he reached the bushes and brambles. Fresh red blood on the ground. Tee could hide his tracks, but not the blood. He must have headed for the timber, a grove of post oak on the hillside. Slocum kept his eyes open and reached the edge, searching the tangle of tree trunks. On his haunches, he could make out the disturbed leaves and a crossed violet stem on the ground. His quarry had gone in there, perhaps to draw him into a trap. Slocum was no fool; he wouldn't be outwitted in the game of cat and mouse. With care and his gun ready, he moved to the right. The smell of spent powder in his nose, he held the gun close to his face, hoping for a flicker of movement.

Sawbriar vines forced him to detour more to the side, his vision glued on the steep hill above him. Higher up some room-sized rocks might conceal his man. No telling how far or how strong he was after being shot the night before—still he came back for revenge.

A figure appeared on the biggest outcropping, and smoke came from the muzzle of his gun. Slocum hit the deck. Bark flew and leaves were cut down in a shower. On his stomach, he used both hands to take aim and emptied his .45 at the figure. The last two made the target jerk as if hit, and then he pitched forward off the rock. Landing on his back after a twenty-foot fall, he slid downhill ten feet or so, before he managed to roll over and begin to crawl for cover.

His Colt reloaded, Slocum yelled at him to stop. But turtle-like he kept on, and Slocum took aim. His first shot shattered bark over him as a warning. The killer kept crawling. Slocum's next shot stopped him and he collapsed face-down. Getting his breath, Slocum leaned against a rough-barked oak and reloaded.

A big yawn gapped his mouth as he slipped new rounds in the chamber. This deal was finally over, he might sleep all day, but many a *stilled* sidewinder could manage to bite his enemy before he died. He squatted on his heels and watched for any movement. Though he was facedown fifty feet up-hill, Tee's outstretched right hand still held his handgun—whether he could use it or not was the question.

Slocum eased himself up a step at a time, staying to the right, figuring if Tee rolled over it would be in that direction and he'd have to bring the gun across his body to shoot at him. No sound, no movement; in the distance a mule brayed and honked. Slocum swept a spiderweb out of his face with his left hand.

Then, in fury, Tee spun on his back, making a hate-filled face, but the strength in his gun arm had expired and he couldn't raise the pistol high enough.

"Drop it or die." Slocum aimed his gun at the dark face with white teeth clenched and lips pulled back to expose them. A shaft of sunshine danced on the gold earring, and Tee at last dropped the gun out of his fingers and collapsed on his back.

In three long steps, Slocum kicked it away and looked down at the man. "Smith easy to capture?"

"That . . ." He coughed and blood appeared in the corner of his mouth. "The guy you sent to find . . . me?"

"Yeah, I thought he was tough."

"He was—got a knife in my leg." Then Tee smiled and choked again. "Not as tough as you, huh?"

"Where's the others?"

"You'll have to find them—Henny's killing ugly women, I bet . . . the colonel's . . . screwing them in Fort Worth."

"Where's Henny?"

"Try Goose Creek—" His laughter cut off. He jerked from head to toe in death throes, and his entire body shook like he was trying to ward off the inevitable; then his brown eyes flew open like he'd seen the fires of hell—he stared forever at the circling buzzards.

"That's him," she said, out of breath, looking down at him.

"He said that Smith got a knife in him. Must be his left leg; it looks bandaged under his pants."

She nodded. "He say anything else?"

"Henny may be on Goose Creek."

"Where's that?"

"In the Seneca country," Hurricane said, using a tree for support on the steep hillside and looking at the dead man.

Slocum agreed and nodded. "He said the colonel was in Fort Worth."

"Will Blue wear his gold earring?" she asked.

"I bet she would." Hurricane bobbed his head and squatted, using a tree trunk for support.

"You can have it for her."

He nodded as if in deep thought. "I wonder how many people will rejoice over his death."

"Many at Choteau," Slocum said, bent over and searching the dead man's vest. He tossed out two federal badges. "Bet those men were his victims."

"Yes," Hurricane agreed. "I bet their families would like to know too."

"This was Smith's," Slocum said, pulling out the large elk tooth. "Supposed to bring you luck."

"He used all his; so did Tee," Hurricane said. "Let's drag him down to the foot of the hill. The Fort Smith law may pay a bounty for him with those two badges in his pocket."

"They might." Slocum pocketed some change he found, then took off both of Tee's boots. He smiled at the paper money that fluttered out of them. "He sure wasn't broke."

"I'd say there's several hundred dollars here." Wink bent over and began gathering it.

"It's half Hurricane's and half ours. No telling the source. Hurricane's going to take the body in and get that reward too."

"Must be my lucky day." The Cherokee smiled. "I'll be so damned rich women won't ever leave me alone."

"May not," Slocum agreed as they began to drag Tee off the hillside.

"Buzzards sure want him." Hurricane indicated the birds overhead.

"Yeah, but they don't pay any bounty." Slocum laughed.

They caught their breath at the foot of the hill. Wink ran to get them a horse to carry the body to the cabin.

"You need me to get Henny?" Hurricane asked.

"No, I think we can handle him. I hope we get there before he's murdered too many women."

"Then you going to Texas?"

"I guess that's her plan—she wants the ones killed her son and husband. He said the colonel is down there screwing whores in Fort Worth."

"Long as his money lasts, right?"

"Long as it lasts," Slocum agreed, and in those cases it usually didn't last long.

Wink led a horse back, and they hoisted the body over it to take to the house. Once there, Blue brought them out an old blanket and they wrapped Tee in it. The cover roped on good, Slocum and Hurricane left him on the porch, washed their hands and joined the women for breakfast.

"Black Fox is the name of the man I know up there," Hurricane said, passing the tin pan piled high with biscuits.

"What's he do?"

"Good medicine man—he could tell you if Henny is up there."

"Where can we find him?"

"He has a farm. He will tell you if Henny is in that country."

"I'll find him. Anything else?"

Hurricane shook his head, but his eyes looked in deep meditation. "Be careful. The least mean dog can bite the hardest of them all."

"We'll heed your advice." He looked over at Wink and she nodded too.

"When will we leave?" she asked.

"Going to rain this afternoon. Better wait till in the morning."

Wink smiled at him. "Glad you thought of that."

"He needs some sleep anyway." Hurricane shrugged at her.

Busy eating his biscuits and gravy, Slocum smiled to himself. He might be in bed the rest of the day—but not sleeping.

11

Sunlight shone through the cracks in the wall of the shed and danced on her snowy bare tits that quaked in motion. Slocum held her hips in his grasp as she raised and lowered herself on his stiff pole. A smile came across her face each time she went down and the ropes under the goose-down mattress creaked in protest. With the side of her hand she swept the curls back from her face and used the fingertips of her other hand to push off for balance.

"This sure beats mopping floors and waiting on old women who can't make their minds up."

"Guess you and him never . . . ?"

"Never what?" Her hand flew to her mouth and she blushed. "We did it under covers even in the heat of the summertime, with most of our clothes on. I think Walter was afraid to look at me naked."

"Really?"

"He wouldn't look at me taking a bath. I wondered if his first wife had been pretty; then one day I discovered an old tintype of her and she was short and very fat—kinda barrel-shaped. Walter never would talk about her. He hardly talked to me except about store business. The first night he said,

'This is what married people do. I'll try not to hurt you, but it will, so don't cry'."

"Did it hurt?"

"For a second—but I was lost and didn't know anything except animals did it. I really thought barnyard animals had more fun doing it than we did." She bent over and kissed him, then whispered. "You need to finish this business."

They changed positions, and in minutes their rasping breath reached new heights. His organ swelled to greater proportions, and her walls began to contract in spasms. Then from the depths of his scrotum came the charge that sent her into oblivion, as thunder rolled over the cabin's roof

Raindrops began to patter on the roof, then the rap of small hail. Eyes closed and body limp underneath him, she moaned. "Gawd, if Walter had ever known."

They left before daylight. All the vegetation dripped water, but they pushed north hard with their pack mule in tow. Two ferry crossings and by late afternoon they were in the country where Tee said they'd find Henny. A storekeeper directed them to Black Fox, and they reached his place as the sun died in a fiery ball.

A gray-headed man wearing short braids came to the lighted door and nodded.

"Hurricane Wilson sent us to see you," Slocum said, leaning on his saddle horn.

"If you are his friend, you are welcome here. Get down and put your horses up. We have much food and look for your company."

"We're here," Slocum said to Wink, and she smiled, more in relief than from being pleased; he realized he'd pushed it hard all day to reach this place.

Fox took a candle lamp and showed them the pen with plenty of hay in the rack.

He squatted down as they unloaded. "You came long ways today."

"I didn't want the one we look for to know we are here. Henny Williams," Slocum said.

Fox shook his head. "I know of no one by that name."

"He is a real skinny cowboy, kinda stoop-shouldered," she said, peeling the tarp off the packs. "Big nose and large mouth."

"Calls himself Joseph Wall now."

Slocum nodded and set his saddle on end. "He around here?"

"Maybe ten miles over, at Big Shoat."

"He's bad about murdering women," Wink said.

"Huh?"

"That's what he's wanted for," she said.

"Two Indian women been killed in the last few weeks. No one knows why or who did it."

"He'd be your chief suspect. He's a woman killer," said Slocum.

Fox nodded. "I am glad that Hurricane sent you. I will send my son to find some leaders and have you tell them about this man."

"Be glad to," Slocum said.

Fox's wife's name was unpronounceable—so they called her Choe. A bright-faced woman, her beauty was well preserved in a society and way of life that took its toll on pretty females. Choe made them fry bread, and they ate it filled with slow-fire-cooked beef chunks, gravy and green beans. Slocum knew he had eaten too much, but he shook his head. "Why is he not fatter—your cooking is too good."

She beamed and shook her head. "This is company food—I feed him cold cornbread."

"See why I was so glad you came," Fox said and smiled at Wink.

His teenage boy, who had ridden out earlier, returned with three men—all Indians. They came inside and nodded, taking seats that Choe found for them.

"He is a friend of Hurricane who comes here to find a

man kills woman," Fox said and introduced the men. White Bear was the tallest, Red Hawk the oldest, with a deeply eroded, wrinkled face, and Come-Back, in his twenties, the only one with a conventional haircut.

"He and others murdered my son and husband in Kansas," she said and passed the poster around.

"The one they described is like Joseph Wall. See there, he has killed women before, it says on the poster."

They nodded. "What should we do? Wait for the marshal to send someone?" Red Hawk asked.

"I'll arrest him and take him in if he doesn't try anything. He goes to shooting, I'll collect the bounty," Slocum said.

"What is the bounty?" White Bear reached over for the poster and studied it. "One hundred dollars, hmm."

"The money is not important. He was with the men killed her boy."

"I think we should go and ask him about the murder of the Seneca woman and my cousin Dora," White Bear said.

The others agreed.

"When?" Slocum asked.

"Now."

"Fine. I will saddle my horse and go along." Slocum turned and looked at Wink as he rose. "You better stay here."

She agreed. "I'll keep Choe company."

Slocum saddled Red and soon led him out to join the Indians. The bay nickered at him when he mounted and they rode off. Under a quarter moon they went through the open farmland and over the post-oak-clad hills. The country they entered was more rolling hills in tall bluestem, and soon went down a long, deep draw that was watered by a spring that flowed over the limestone rock ledges.

When they halted, Fox pointed out a cabin and some pens. In the night, an owl hooted and the soft wind swept a soft song though the grass on the ridges. They dismounted and hitched their horses to some scrub brush. With their guns, they spread out at the base and Red Hawk sent White

Bear to get close—obviously he was the quietest man, despite his size.

Time ticked slow; Slocum shifted his weight from one leg to the other while squatted with the others. Then their scout shouted for them to come and lighted a lamp inside so they could see.

"Something is wrong," Black Fox said as they hurried downhill.

Slocum agreed.

They filed into the small one room, and Slocum could see the thick brown legs and bare ass of an Indian woman lying on the quilts on the bed, surrounded by men. Her body had been badly mutilated with a knife by a madman.

"I'm sorry I came too late," Slocum said to them, pursed his lips and shook his head.

"When did this happen?" Black Fox asked.

"A day ago," an older man said. "Her killer is long gone."

"What will you do now?" Fox asked Slocum.

"He is not a ghost. A man leaves tracks, signs. I'll follow him until I find him."

The solemn-faced men nodded in the flickering candle-light.

"Why does he kill women?" Come-Back asked.

"He's not man enough to kill a man," Red Hawk said. "He is sick and there is no way to ever cure him except kill him—he will kill again and again until someone does. May you have success finding this mad one." He clapped Slocum on the arm.

"I'll need it," Slocum said.

They left Black Fox and Choe after a day of rest and a chance to fix a shoe on Wink's bay. He took a northwest course after White Bear came by and said the Henny had gone that way. Perhaps to follow the Arkansas River; so Slocum headed for Wichita.

A storekeeper across the line remembered him. "Yeah, he

was riding a thin paint and leading a gray and coyote-colored one."

"Agouti," Slocum said and nodded. "He say where he was headed?"

"Talked about Fort Dodge."

That might be a ploy, but not many men rode a paint and led a gray and coyote-colored horse. He tipped his hat to the man, and carried out the sack of hard candy for her he'd paid for.

"He been here?" she asked, smiling at his gift. "Thanks."

"You needed something; we still got a long haul."

'Have I ever complained or slacked?"

"No, ma'am, and don't start now." He threw a leg over Red and they went north.

He left her at the hotel at Wichita and checked out several of the saloons around cow town, or what was left of the old cattle shipping area. The herds had gone farther west by this time—tick fever and honyockers plowing up the grass. They were even talking prohibition in Kansas. No place for a cowboy—though they were grateful for a hot bath, a good meal and a night in a real bed to frolic. They rode on the next day.

West of Wichita, a crossroads storekeeper, sweeping off his porch, scratched his bushy sideburns and nodded at Slocum's questions. *Had he seen a man on a paint horse? A skinny cowboy?*

"Went through here two days ago. Going west."

Slocum tipped his hat to the man, then looked at her. She nodded with a grim look and booted the bay on.

The homesteads grew farther apart. Soddies with rusty stovepipes. Hill corn on once sod land roughly plowed and sheaths rustling in the dry wind. Late afternoon they stopped at a place, hoping to buy a meal. The door was open when Slocum knocked with no answer. No one in the sparsely furnished room when he stuck his head inside to check.

"No one's here."

Still in the saddle, she narrowed her eyes and searched

across the rolling country. "Why go away and leave the door open?"

"Three horses been here," he said and knelt to study the tracks in the matted grass.

"We better search around." She booted her horse for the draw. After a check around the homestead, he swung into the saddle and turned at her call.

"Slocum, come quick. We're too late."

He drove Red to where she sat her horse and was trying to look away. Reined up short, he saw the naked woman's body in the grass. The stark, bare white skin against the still-red blood all over her carved torso—sprawled on her back—a young woman, in her teens.

"Why must he kill them?" she screamed and broke into tears.

"I don't know." He dismounted and handed her the reins. "We've got to bury her."

"Where is her man? Children?"

"No way of knowing. All we can do is bury her and leave a note."

"I'm sorry. It is getting to me."

"Me too, Wink, me too." He lifted the young woman's body in his arms, trying to ignore the damage to her.

Wink rode to the house, dismounted and burst inside. She returned, blinking against the sun, with a worn green blanket. On her knees she fought the wind to spread it out for him with a head shake. "They sure ain't got much, have they?"

With care he laid the blanket out and they wrapped the girl in it. He shoved off his knees to go and look for a shovel. Long past dark, he said a short prayer over her. Then he covered her up.

Wink made some cornbread in a skillet with red beans, and they ate in the silence of some flickering mutton-fat candles that emitted a strong sheep aroma in the room.

"I ain't sure what's the worst—cooking with dry cowpies or them candles," she said.

"I can't help you," he said and shook his head half-amused.

To whom it may concern,

A killer rode by here and murdered your wife. We are on his trail but so far he has avoided capture—his name is Henny Williams. But he uses other names. We paused and gave her a Christian funeral and pray that you will find some solace in that arrangement.

J. Slocum

They left the next morning and rode on for Dodge. Somehow the death of the young woman had taken the fun out of their travels; they both acted downcast and spent the day in their own minds crossing the prairie. Slocum wondered if he'd only pushed harder, maybe they could have saved her. Wink seemed locked up in her own guilt, and when they found a small place with a store, saloon and freight yard, they stopped before sundown.

The saloon man told Slocum to bring "his wife" inside, that no one would embarrass her, and he had some fresh steaks he'd have cooked for them. The prospect of real food restored his energy, and they put the horses in the freight yard.

"Anyone around here see him pass through?" she asked as they came back up the dusty ruts to the saloon in the twilight.

"Guess I never asked."

"Guess it can wait too," she said. She hugged his arm and laid her forehead on his shoulder. "Hold me for minute before we go in there."

"I could do it all night."

"No, we'd miss those steaks he promised you."

"You know," he said, "you're right."

12

Slocum knew all about it—he'd been there as an army scout, a buff hunter and a drover. Southwest Kansas hosted the booming queen of the cow towns, Dodge City. It was situated on the north side of the dwindling Arkansas River that by late summer a man could piss in and raise the water level. Cattle shipping yards, whores—fat ones, thin ones, pretty ones, Mexican ones for the Latinos and black ones for anyone with two bits and a stiff prick—Dodge had been the Army's supply point until the Cheyennes and the rest of the red devils were herded out of the area to make room for dirt farmers to starve. It served as the buffalo hide center for the scourge of hunters decimating the woolly bastards as fast as they could shoot them. The whores there in those early days were mostly diseased Indian wenches that serviced customers anywhere handy—on a stinging hide pile, in the back of a wagon, in the alley, and one Arapaho teen even took on six shooters in a row on top of a pool table in Scott's Saloon one afternoon. Filthy, dirty, and the clap running out of their cunts in rivers down their dirt-crusted legs—many a black soldier cried every time he tried to piss and couldn't, *That no-account red bitch!* And some hide hunter, equally afflicted, said worse.

But Dodge had cleaned up its act—no guns, no fucking whores in public, a brothel inspector who certified that the employees of each cathouse were disease free. They tried to run off the streetwalkers and close down the independents that didn't buy a license and pay the "tax." But Dodge still ran wide open night and day. Men still shot each other despite the gun law, and a young drover fresh up the trail from Texas could, after four months' hard work, lose his virginity, his money and all else he owned in a few hours and turn up dead in a back alley.

Herds were spread out for miles grazing, waiting for the next cars to be spotted, a higher bid or the boss man considering running them up to Montana and a better market. Slocum and Wink rode around them. He asked a drover or two they met if they'd seen a cowboy on a paint horse. That usually drew a laugh—no self-respecting cowboy ever rode a paint horse. No, they had not seen him.

Slocum was beginning to wonder if Henny had given them the slip, when he came across Simms Wilson, an older trail boss he knew from his days on the drives.

"They ain't kilt you yet?" Wilson grinned and then took off his hat for her with a nod. "You're in tough company, ma'am." He spat tobacco aside.

"I know," she said and smiled.

"Your herd sold?" Slocum asked, holding his saddle horn and looking over the grazing longhorns.

Wilson shook his head. "I may need some blankets and a thick coat too. Market's down."

"Good luck. I'm looking for guy riding a paint and leading two other dinks he stole in the Nation."

"Oh, bejesus, be bad to be hung for horse rustling, but for stealing a pinto—that would be a damn shame—excuse me, ma'am. My language ain't too good after all this time on the trail." He leaned over on the far side and spat again, wiping his mustached mouth on his sleeve. "Hey, come to think of it, he was in Dodge yesterday. I about forgot. What did he do besides steal them Injun horses?"

"Murdered several women and shot her son and husband in a robbery."

"Hell, he needs hung,"

"He needs stopped."

"Better go by the sheriff and all them marshals. They don't like no gunplay unless it's their own."

"I'll go see them."

"Good. Hope you get him. And, ma'am, I'm sure sorry about your loss."

She nodded that she heard him and they rode on.

Their horses in the livery, they took a hotel room and a bath. She wore her new dress and they ate in a fine restaurant. A tall man with a mustache, in a black suit, came over and nodded. "Evening, Slocum, didn't expect to see you in these parts."

"Virgil Earp, like you to meet Wink Trent."

Virgil took off his hat and bowed to her. "My pleasure, ma'am."

"Let him see that wanted poster," Slocum said, and she drew it from her handbag.

"A gang held up her store over east of here in Kansas, shot her husband and son. One of their members is in Dodge or was yesterday. He was riding a paint he stole down in the Nation."

"Murdered women?" Virgil frowned looking at the wanted sheet.

"He murdered one three days ago east of here. We buried her."

"Cuts them all up?"

"Yes, did he murder one here?"

Virgil nodded. "Some dove last night, and it was a bad mess. I need to get word out to everyone. Thanks." He handed the poster back. "Nice to meet you, ma'am."

In a rush, Virgil hurried out the door and shouted to someone, but Slocum couldn't hear him.

"Will they get him?" she asked.

"Maybe. We'll stick around and be certain."

"Good. That's a nice bed up there."

"I bet it is."

The next morning the *Dodge Gazette* headlined the "woman killer" story. Henny's three animals remained under surveillance in the Keystone Wagon Yard; the owner did not appear to claim them. Slocum shook his head—and furthermore he wouldn't go back and get them either, if he could read. The biggest question was which way did Henny go, and without the paint he'd be much harder to identify. North, south, east, or west? Damn, Slocum wished he'd waited and located him before telling the law—Virgil Earp was the best one of the brothers, but even he had sent Henny rushing off.

How many more women would he kill? That's what ate at Slocum's guts. Each one would be on his conscience. Damn.

"What now?" she asked after he explained the whole thing to her at breakfast.

"We need a lead on where he went."

"How do we get that?"

"Ask a lot of folks. You can try the stores and women. I'll try other places. Even a hint would help—someone saw him last."

It was past noon when they met back at the hotel room.

"You do any good?" he asked, turning when she entered the door.

"Maybe—a swamper at the store said he thought Henny left with some women in a wagon."

"Which way?"

"West, I guess."

"We should catch a wagon in a day if we ride hard. He say anything about them?"

"Not much. Said they had some big mules pulling it and they were from Missouri."

"We better ride. He's liable to kill all three of them."

They threw their things together and hurried to the stables. Slocum hired the hand to help them load their horses and mule, and they soon rode west from Dodge. In a few hours, they met the great ball of fire in the west and decided to camp on the river before nightfall, out of fear they'd miss or go past the wagon in the darkness.

Before dawn, they broke camp and headed west again. The road followed the river like the railroad tracks did, and by afternoon, sight of the canvas top of a wagon in the cottonwoods had caused them to draw up.

"Be careful," he said to her, and they turned off the road and headed for the campfire smoke.

"Hello the camp," he said aloud, and a woman with a shotgun leveled at him stepped around from behind the wagon.

"Hold it right there," she ordered in a gravel voice of authority. Strands of gray hair hung unpinned from the rest and her eyes were dark as coals.

"Is he here?" he asked.

"Who's he?"

"Henny Williams, a skinny fellow—"

"No. You a friend of his?" She used the gun muzzle to punctuate her words.

"No, ma'am." He motioned to Wink. "He shot her husband and boy."

"Well, that scallywag done stole our good mules and ran off last night."

"He hurt any of you?"

"Why, he'd tried, we'd've whupped his ass for him. That skinny roach—"

"Well, he's murdered several woman. We'll see if we can't run him down and get your animals back."

"I don't know who you two are or your business, mister, but I hope you nail his sorry hide to the outhouse wall when you find him. We would be beholding to you if you could get Molly and Bob back for us."

"Praise the Lord," a toothless older woman said, armed with a single-shot .22 as she climbed down from the tailgate.

"We'd even kill an old fat Dominicker hen," a fat girl in her early twenties said and came around from the far side with a shotgun. "If'n you can find 'em."

"Can't guarantee anything. But we'll ride ahead."

"Ain't they a fort west of here?" the middle one asked.

"Bent's Trading Post. But it's a hundred miles. We'll go that far. We're not back in a week, you three better start out or plan to winter here."

"I got it in my mind you'll get us our mules back." The middle one nodded with a grim set to her thin lips. Then she went over all the details about the mules: how tall they were, scars, weren't broke to ride, age, unshod.

"What were those women's names?" Wink asked, looking back when they headed west again and were out of earshot.

"I ain't sure they ever said, but old Henny met his match with them." They both laughed.

"We know more about the mules than we do the women."

"Two bay mules, sixteen hands, old wire-cut scar on the mare mule's left leg."

"Molly and Bob. That's the mules' names. How far can he get on a mule like that?" Wink asked.

"To hell and back, but he'll earn every mile. They weren't saddle broke, he just found the one could be ridden."

"Can we catch him this side of the fort?"

"Maybe."

Dark, they made camp and gathered some chips and a little wood for a cooking fire before twilight faded. Then she cooked them beans that took forever to soften. Somewhere in the night a coyote gave bray and Slocum turned an ear. In the distance, he heard a mule bray. He ran to their pack animal and muzzled him to prevent him answering.

"What's wrong?" she asked, out of breath and joining him.

"There's mule not a half mile away."

"Reckon it's him?"

"Only way to know is go find out. I'll need to do it on foot—mules gone to braying at my horse will warn him. You have to keep this one quiet too, so he don't get suspicious and move on."

"Be careful. Maybe the beans will be done by the time you get back."

They both laughed and he kissed her on the cheek.

Starlight shone on the vast sagebrush-bunchgrass sea as he made his way in a jog down the road. He caught his breath on the next rise and listened—nothing but the night insects creaking. Another half mile, he stopped in his tracks. Off to his left, in the trees along the river, he heard a horse or mule cough. Almost went by them.

The outlines of three animals stood hipshot in the shadowy light. Two were large mules and the other a mustang. Slocum squatted down to get the lay of the camp. A small fire still smoked, the bitter fumes on the night's soft breeze.

One bedroll to the side—someone looked rolled up in it. With care to be sure there wasn't anyone else in camp, Slocum made his way around the site and came in with the river to his back. Then he stepped up, pistol in hand and shoved it in the man's ear.

"Move a twitch and you're dead."

"Huh?"

"Where's Henny?" he demanded and jerked the covers back. Then he got the man up by using his free hand, so he couldn't reach for weapon, and checked him for one.

"Who?"

"The mule rustler?" Satisfied the short man behind the beard wasn't his man, Slocum continued his interrogation.

"I-I never stole them mules. Bought them."

"They were rustled."

"I sure never—"

"What's your name?"

"Watts, why?"

"Well, Watts, the three women who own them mules are stranded east of here. Where did he go?"

"West, I guess. I paid him twenty apiece and give him a good pony in trade."

Slocum looked at the stars in that direction. Time he got the mules back to those sisters and got on Henny's track again, there was no telling how far he'd get. Damn.

"Break camp. We have a long ways to go."

"I never knowed he was a rustler," Watts said, rolling up his bedroll. "I swear I never knowed that—"

"He also killed a lot of women."

"How many?"

"About a dozen I can account for."

"Why kill a woman?"

"Don't like 'em I guess. Move. We've got lots to do."

"Holy cow—I offered him to sleep here tonight." The man still acted shook over the whole thing. "I never—what you going to do to me?"

"Maybe those women will offer you a reward—I can't promise. They'll be glad to see their mules."

Watts rubbed his throat. "Sounds good to me."

It was close to dawn when Slocum and his bunch reached the women's camp. Mother met them with a shotgun and eyed them critically in the half-light.

"Those your mules?" Slocum asked, dismounting.

"Damn sure are."

"Good, you owe Mr. Watts any reward you planned to offer for their return."

Her eyes narrowed like slits, she shoved the shotgun at Slocum. "Them mules were stolen. How do we know he wasn't in on the plan?"

"'Cause Henny got forty dollars and a good horse out of him in trade for them."

"I reckon we'd pay ten dollars."

"It's a big loss to him."

"Money don't grow on trees."

"I ain't saying it does. The man was out lots of money; he could've taken those mules and sold them for profit and you'd've never seen them again."

"All right, I'll give him his forty dollars. Kitty, get him the money."

"Coming," the fat girl said, digging in a purse and standing behind the seat.

"Amen, amen," Granny said and climbed out of the back tailgate.

Watts shook Slocum's hand, then booted his horse in close to take the money. "Thanks. You're a square shooter."

"Just watch who you buy mules from in the future."

"Thank you, ma'am," he said to Kitty and took the gold coins from her. "I will. I sure will."

"I never thought we'd ever see them again," she said with wet lashes.

"Proud you have them," he said, acting uneasy in her company.

Then she threw her arms around him and hugged the shorter man, about to smother him. Red-faced, he looked like a man drowning.

"You'll have to stay for—" She blinked her wet eyes as if to see the time of day.

"I reckon since you asked—"

"Oh, yes," she said and steered him around the wagon to the campfire like she owned him.

"Shotgun" made a face of disapproval and then came over to Slocum. "I guess you're in a hurry. Hope you find that slinking dog and skin him alive."

"We're moving on." Slocum stepped in the stirrup and, once seated, saluted her.

"You never said what I owed you."

"Nothing." He turned his horse and motioned for Wink to leave.

"I'll get even with you!" she shouted and he nodded as they trotted west—a good day behind their man, mounted on a bay mustang with an SU brand on his right shoulder, according to Watts.

Bent's Trading Post looked like a flagship in the ocean of gray brown against a curtain of green cottonwoods along the Arkansas. The thickly plastered adobe walls towered over them, and an assortment of freight wagons, ambulances, two-wheel carts, travois-laden Indian ponies all stood around outside the great wooden doors that had not been shut in years.

For years this had been the first sign of civilization for those headed west. The Bent Brothers, married to Cheyenne women, had held a stiff business from the days of the mountain men to present times. For years their business with partner St. Vrain was fur trading with the Plains Indians. One of their satellites was the famous adobe walls site on the Canadian. At the main post, they traded foot-sore oxen for fresh ones for ten to twenty dollars per head depending on the market. The weak ones were turned out to recover and to be swapped later to another teamster needing one.

First place since Missouri for the traveler to buy things like coffee, flour, cornmeal, dry beans and sugar. Most of the goods were freighted up from Santa Fe, before the railroad. At one time, much earlier, the mountain men brought beaver pelts there, and they were baled and sent by mule to St. Louis.

So when he and Wink walked in under the archway, Slocum knew this was hallowed ground in the minds of several old men. Many a camp squaw had been bartered for or bought here. Most were captives and made a good item to trade for firewater. Slocum could recall sitting on his haunches as six Cheyenne bucks, not out of their teens, brought in five young women—Crows.

Their buffalo ponies no longer danced on their toes— gaunt from the hard miles they had pushed them, they blew exhausted in the dust. Some no doubt fed the ravens and coyotes where they had fallen headfirst to the ground, unable to be flailed by quirt into another step. Two girls to a pony, wrists tied in front and then looped together by the braided leather nooses, a short lead that forced them to dismount at the same time or strangle one another.

One pair of girls' sea legs failed to hold them up once off the pony, and they spilled on their butts. One of the captors ran over and jerked both to their feet by a handful of hair, shoving them to the circle they had set for them to be held in. His rawhide boots slapping around his rock-hard calves and his shoulders wide like an eagle after prey, he drove them to the others. Under his breath, he called them whores and worthless in his own language.

It took no imagination to think how the six boys had shown their manhood by raping each of the girls repeatedly on the long journey south. Jerking the chosen one up by the hair from the circle and dragging her into the shadows of night; forcing her down on the sharp sticks, where he'd unceremoniously whip up her short skirt, spread her knees, without regard, and penetrate her cunt, jacking it to her until he came deep inside her and then laughed and mocked her.

They came to this place to trade their prizes. In the next two days, they sold two for slaves to a don taking them to Sante Fe. He took the thickest ones. His desire was for ones that could work—his segundo took them to his camp on the river, and Slocum never saw them again. The man in the gold-braided vest paid the head boy eighty gold dollars for them. The six boys were not stupid—they understood the worth of money well.

That night two freighters sat at their fire, and the bucks stripped the four who were left naked and made them model for the two whiskered men old enough to be their grandfathers, who slobbered looking at them. Full of firewater, the teamsters chose two of the budding teenagers and paid sixty dollars and four gallons of whiskey for them. The two white men took their purchases and quickly left the camp as soon as the trade was finalized.

The one in charge put three gallons of the whiskey away after much arguing and allowed them only one to drink. It was enough. All night they war danced and then they took turns openly screwing the remaining two girls. Sometimes two would screw a single one at same time. Afterward, they would laugh and clap each other on the shoulder standing naked in the red firelight, their erections shrunk away and their belief that they were world conquerors filling their expanded chests. Had they not came to this big place with plenty of white men about to see them, riding stolen fancy horses and bringing a bevy of handsome captives to sell for high prices?

The next day they lay about hungover, and only a few lookers came to poke at the filthy, disheveled girls, who looked as bad as their captors. But by afternoon the leader had made two of them bucks take the pair to the river and wash them. He went and found a squaw who sewed and bought two buckskin shirts from her that would make them short dresses.

Slocum had watched the young leader unbraid the whole lot of them. No more sex with them. They must look nice-looking for the buyers—even the dumb, horny white men did not want soiled merchandise.

The next day some packers came in and grinned big at the young teenage merchandise. The leader sold one to them for a Henry rifle, a cap-and-ball pistol and seventy dollars in gold.

The last one was probably the youngest, since she had only budding breasts. But another white-whiskered man came and traded for her—he dragged her off like a cur dog on a leash. Slocum never knew what he gave for her, but the Cheyenne in charge was no fool, despite his youth.

Their leader had swapped his tired horses for fresh mounts, and some furs they'd brought for three more rifles and ammo—so each one had a rifle or pistol. They left the fort for parts north howling like wild men, and Bent's returned to being a place where a Frenchman could get drunk, stand on a crate in the square and give a sermon in his own language on the stupidity of the Americans.

Slocum wondered about the six bucks and whatever happened to them. A few years later a Crow told him the story about the abductors' fate. Three Crows had trailed them from Montana to southeast Colorado. They snuck up one night and put poison mushrooms in the three whiskey crocks, then sat back and waited.

Four died from drinking it, in pain and with much suffering; they paid for what they did to the Crow girls. The leader and one more never drank, so they survived. The younger one died at the Rose Bud Battle, and a short week later the leader, who called himself Red Blanket, shot George Armstrong Custer in the chest at the edge of the Little Bighorn River, with the same pistol he'd traded a Crow woman for at Bent's Fort.

In the too bright noon sun, Wink sat beside Slocum on the bench and they drank the sharp tomato juice from an opened airtight before spearing out the red fruit. It was a good treat, and each had an unopened can of peaches for dessert. Indian women crossed the open square hauling things on their backs from a band on their foreheads. Other groups of them sat aside in the shade and gossiped in their own language like magpies.

Some freighters used their rifles for posts to lean on as they talked with others about the road or the business. Perhaps they shared some news about the Indian wars that raged miles from there, or the economy and banking.

"Learn anything?" she asked him.

"No one's seen him or anyone like his description."

"Maybe he went elsewhere?"

"I am thinking that too."

A salt-and-pepper bearded man in dirty buckskins came over and put his Winchester brass butt on the bench. "They say you're looking for a skinny cowboy riding a shaggy mustang."

"You see him?"

"This morning, headed west."

"Going toward Santa Fe?"

The man nodded. "What'd he do?"

"Murdered several woman."

"I hope you get him then." He nodded as if satisfied, lifted his rifle and went on.

"What should we do now?" she asked under her breath.

"Board the horses and catch a passenger train to Santa Fe."

"You serious?"

"Dead serious."

"What if he—"

"We miss him, we miss him. Try again."

"I'm ready, Boss."

They caught the evening passenger service at Sidler's Switch. The telegrapher put out a red lantern, and the train stopped in a screech of steel on steel and a hiss of the air brakes. A conductor put down a step at the back of the second car and waved them on there. Once they were aboard, he tossed the step on and waved his lamp at the engineer. They were on the platform when the shock of the engine starting gave them a jerk and they had to grab for something or be thrown down. In minutes, their small amount of baggage was in a rack overhead and they had a seat in the back of the dimly lighted car.

The night fled by at twenty-five miles an hour; a strong stench of burning coal caught in the car once in a while, and the lonesome whistle marked each crossing, wailing off in the night to the howls of coyotes that answered it. A clack-clack sounded over the seams, and the car swayed like a boat. By mid-morning they had reached the Santa Fe siding station, where they took a coach the ten miles to town, across the piñon-juniper mesa to the ancient, sleepy adobe settlement set at the base of the mountains.

They found a room in a two-story hotel, with a balcony that overlooked the square. If Henny rode in, Slocum wanted to see him—everyone who came there rode into the plaza; it was the hub of the city, and all roads led there. So did the double freight wagons pulled by eighteen head of bullocks, and the squeaky ox carts of the produce farmers from the Rio Grand Valley. The valley split New Mexico north to south like a huge ax blow in the earth, from the deep gorges in the north to the flatter willow bottoms in the south. This city had risen long before the pilgrims came to New England. They still took siestas, and they closed their shops, cantinas and stores every afternoon for the event. It had handicapped Slocum and her when they arrived and wanted a room or anything to eat.

At last the cafés opened, and a waiter took their order in the lacy shade.

"Ah, fresh chicken," the waiter said in Spanish and kissed the ends of his fingers for Wink's benefit. "We have the fresh one today. No rooster for you, these are fat lovely pullets."

"We'll have the chicken," Slocum said. He'd had enough of the sissy waiter, who probably had no balls under the tight-fitting pants.

"Ah, to drink, señor?"

"Wine for her, whiskey for me."

"Yes, I will be right back."

Amused, she saved her smile until they were alone. "You disliked him?"

"I can't stand prissy men."

"Why?"

"You've lived a very sheltered life, my dear. They have sex with other men."

A frown shaded her eyes. "Oh, no."

He looked away at the fine gray horse of a man dressed in a Spanish suit who rode into the square. "There's a powerful stallion. A Barb and a wonderfully gaited animal."

"I must say I think you have the poor waiter all wrong."

"Look at the horse; he's much more pleasing than that strange waiter."

Slocum sat back as the man dismounted and a boy rushed forward to hold the horse. The boy had obviously been positioned there to wait for his patron and be sure nothing happened to the great horse. The man swept onto the patio, and three of the servers were on his coattails, including theirs. They took the man's order for a drink and asked him how he was and how things were out at his hacienda.

"Fine. Doing very well, thank you. What is fresh today?" He was swinging the riding crop around idly, until he at last grasped it in his other hand when his waiter finished the pitch for the fowl.

"Yes, bring the fresh chicken and the usual."

"I don't believe I know you, sir," he said, looking across two empty tables at them.

"Tom White, this is Mrs. White."

"Nice to meet you, madam. New to Santa Fe?"

"We arrived a few hours ago," Slocum said.

"Nice place, the only civilized one this side of San Francisco."

"Yes. I like the Barb stallion you're riding as well."

"He's a handful; not for a man like you, but for me he's really quite a horse."

"You do quite well."

"Excuse me, my good lady, my name is Ralph," He stood up, walked over, took her hand and touched his lips to it. "You are a gem in a large mountainous pile of rocks. Ralph Cardin at your service. May I join you?" He eased into a chair at their table and smiled at Slocum, who nodded his approval.

"You have business here?" Cardin asked.

"A man who killed her husband and son is headed here."

Cardin blinked. "You said you were—"

"We are covering our identity so he doesn't learn we wait here for him."

"And this outlaw is?"

"Henny Williams, a murderer of women as well."

"When will he arrive?"

"In a few days."

Cardin considered Slocum's words, and the waiters delivered the drinks. Alone again, he raised his gaze. "I could send some of my men out to learn where he is at."

"A marshal did that in Dodge and it made the next morning's paper. He hightailed it out of there."

"Oh, señor. My men have closed mouths. No newspaper will learn a thing. He may be at Las Vegas too."

"Could be."

"You look in doubt, señor?"

"Why do that for us?"

"This man is a killer, no?"

"Yes."

"Then we don't need him here in Santa Fe."

Slocum narrowed his gaze at the man. "If they locate him, I want to be in on it."

"No problem."

"Show him the poster," Slocum said and leaned back to sip his whiskey. A golden glow shone through the fine glassware, from a glint of sunlight that managed to spear through the lacy shade. Some things were too good to be true. Why did Slocum distrust this rich man? Maybe his obvious move to get Wink's attention had him off center—Cardin's too quick "I'll help" didn't make sense. There was something in it for him—but Slocum was not certain what.

13

Ralph Cardin's hospitality included them moving to his *casa grande* and staying there, while his men scoured the country for Henny Williams. The land by Santa Fe that Cardin owned had been part of an old land grant, and it was obvious to Slocum that Cardin had not made his money in New Mexico agriculture there—but he did have orchards and lots of produce in the irrigated fields. His cattle operation was on the plains to the east of the mountains, and he also wanted them to see that spread. Slocum choose to stay close, in case one of Cardin's three men made contact with the killer.

He stood in the cool morning air beside the drapes and studied the men getting ready to work the farm. A hatless, gray-headed *segundo* put his hand on each man's shoulder and used his other hand to make waving motions to go with his instructions. Individual, patient attention for each one, and a laugh or two at the end that carried to the open French doorway on the balcony. Many men under him would want his power and the job when he grew too old—but few could mold the workforce like him, make them happy with what they did that day, believing it was worthy, and send them to do another chore tomorrow that the *segundo* saw as needing to be done to keep the whole circle under his command complete. Such leaders were scarce and this neat, well-kept place spoke of his talent—Slocum felt glad he had been able to observe him in action while the day still held the freshness only first light could bring.

Saucy women's voices soon echoed in the courtyard. Two women carried wicker baskets of wash; their words were plain enough—". . . you sleep with such a donkey dick and that is why your back is sore. Work did not cause it to be so." Then more bantering and laughter.

He dressed and eased out, leaving Wink asleep on the fine goose-down bed. They'd shared blankets on the hard ground, slept in sheds and old buildings, but this was better than any hotel or place they'd been in so far. Obviously Cardin wanted to separate them and keep her. It did not matter that she was Slocum's woman—Cardin desired Wink for his own. Like his Barb stallion, he only possessed the best, and even as slightly used merchandise, the woman was a diamond in a sandy wash full of rocks. Something like that. Maybe there would be news that day from Cardin's men about the killer's whereabouts.

"Ah, Señor Slocum, you are awake so early," Nona said when he entered the kitchen. The buxom woman's pleasant smile showed her white teeth, and the genuine goodness sparkled in her brown eyes. "Coffee?"

He nodded, looking over the fresh-plucked chickens on the counter, their skin a bright pink with a yellow cast of grain feed.

"They tell me the help drinks the first pot, and it is the best," he said, taking the steaming mug from her.

"Ah, so the *patrón* never learns that."

"I think he knows, but does not dare complain." He stood in the open back door and studied the activity in the yard.

"Don't tell him, please," she said in a mock-concerned voice.

"I won't. This is a peaceful place. Not many like it are left in this world."

"The old hacienda system was good to the people. But

they were never satisfied; they wanted to own them, and they had no idea how to run them."

Slocum knew the same thing. "That's why so many closed, and the *patrón* took his money and left them there to eat the dust."

"Exactly. Big deal to live like an Apache in a hut. No, I am pleased that we are here with Señor Cardin. Silly ones go away, and then they find they must buy the food, must get the wood to cook it and pay the rent, and they never have anything to show. Then they come back and beg the *segundo* to give them their old job back."

"Does he?"

"Not often. He has much knowledge and can look in their eyes and see the sincere ones."

Slocum sipped the coffee and nodded. He wished one of Cardin's men would return with news.

"I have some eggs, sausage, chopped tomatoes, fresh goat cheese and peppers. Marie is making you some fresh flour tortillas. You wish to eat?"

"Eat? I can always eat." He turned back and went to sit on a tall stool to watch as she deftly dressed the birds.

"Make him breakfast," she said to the young girl who was busy dicing vegetables. "She is just engaged so she may burn things." Then Nona laughed and the girl blushed as she went by her. "Oh, to be young again. Would you like that?"

"Some days I would. But to have the knowledge too?"

"No, no, none of that."

"You set too many boundaries on it."

"You have few. I can tell. You have the eyes of a lobo wolf; you look at everything, appraise your stake in it and then trot off."

"I look that wild?"

She met his gaze and nodded ever so slightly. "Last night you slept with that lovely woman upstairs. Tonight . . ." She shook her head as if to clear it. "Tonight you may sleep in an arroyo with a stone for a pillow. You will be the same."

"The same?"

"You feel little pain. A man like that is a hard one for his enemies to put down."

"But you can see my enemies?"

"One is on a horse and he comes this way."

"Thin, stoop shoulders?"

She laughed and busied herself reaching with her right hand inside the carcass for the guts of the second bird. Soon the bluish spiraling entrails, liver and heart were on the table beside the first one's, and she eased the hollow bird into the kettle of water. A sour gas came with the removal, but it soon dissipated into the room's smells of mesquite smoke, cooking meat and tortilla making.

After a long pause, she nodded. "This is the man you seek?"

"Yes, he's murdered many women, besides her husband and son."

"He is coming."

"Today? Tomorrow?"

She looked away then shook her head as if time had no meaning in the matter. "He is coming."

"*Gracias,*" he said and toasted the cup at her.

"My hands smell of chicken—"

"I can fill it myself."

"Good. You live alone a lot and don't expect anyone to help you."

"That's me." He went to the coffeepot and then turned back before he squatted down to the side of the fireplace. "I appreciate that news."

"I knew you were thinking hard about it."

With a pot holder he poured his coffee and then nodded to the shy girl standing above him with her tray of food. "I'll eat on the counter. Too much. Way too much food."

She shrugged like she could not help it.

"I will try, though."

The food set down, she curtsied and then backed away.

Midday, Wink, Cardin and Slocum lounged in the shady

patio drinking sweet lemonade. At the sounds of a hard-running horse entering the center courtyard, Cardin rose.

"You may have your answer." He nodded to Slocum and headed for the gate.

"That would be nice," Wink said and shared a private look of approval with him.

Cardin hurried off and Slocum stopped her. "This man Cardin wants you," he said under his breath, "I can handle Henny. Stay here."

"I will ride with you. I came with you. When the killers of my son and husband are brought down or in jail—then I will have time for my own life."

"Have it your way."

"You expected him to come, didn't you?"

Slocum nodded. "A *bruja* told me he was coming."

"Who?"

"A witch."

Amused at him, she shook her head and then followed him to the courtyard. The vaquero nodded to them at their approach. His lathered horse danced around him despite some jerks on the bits to settle him down; he was still running the race he'd made to get there. Cardin, his arms folded, waited for them, scuffing the side of his knee-high riding boot sole in the thin dust.

"Montoya says the man that you seek will be in Santa Fe by nightfall."

"Good, I'll find him. *Gracias*," he said to the straight-backed man in the gold braid vest.

"Montoya, Pepe and Altovar will be happy to accompany you. They're very discreet."

"Why not? They must know Santa Fe better than you do," she said.

"Send two along with me. I don't want to spook him away."

"Montoya, you and Altovar help him," Cardin said.

"Wear some old clothes," Slocum said. "That nice outfit might warn him."

"We will. Where shall we meet you?" Montoya asked.

"Get a booth in the Isabella Cantina. I will join you there."

"*Sí*, Isabella's." The man nodded to his boss and led the hot horse away to the stables.

"I have an old sombrero I can loan you," Cardin said.

"Make it two," she said and headed back for the house.

"She's not serious, is she?" Cardin blinked his eyes in disbelief at Slocum.

"Sounded serious to me. She's had one thing on her mind since that gang stormed in her store and shot her family—that's seeing they all answered for it."

"But this could be dangerous."

"She's been there. You won't discourage her. I've tried. Three of that gang are pushing up daisies, and the other two soon will be if she has her way."

"A hard side to a beautiful woman. A black widow, no?"

"No, they kill their own."

"But she is such a lovely woman. How can she?"

"I thought that the hot day in Kansas when she hired me. Thought she'd get bogged down in this business and quit." Slocum shook his head. "She's not going to, and she can outshoot many men."

"But it is one thing to shoot a tin can . . ."

"And another to shoot an outlaw busting outside with his gun blazing at you."

"She didn't?"

"Oh, yes."

"I hope your plan goes well and no one is hurt tonight. My men are as tough as any."

"Your *segundo* hired them?"

Cardin blinked. "You have met Valdez?"

"No, but I have watched him. You are very fortunate to have him. Such men are rare these days."

"You amaze me. You infiltrate my casa and know all about everything. Come, I can use a strong drink."

Slocum looked around. The place was calm again, save for the plodding of one horse. A small brown-skinned boy, barefooted, led the nearly dry bay back and forth at a respectable distance. Caked-on salt frosted his chest and shoulders. He occasionally dropped his head and coughed.

"There is no *donna* here?" Slocum asked.

"Not for many years. Louise died over a decade ago, and I thought no one could ever fill that gap."

Slocum nodded.

"She was on a stage. Apaches attacked it south of Socorro. She'd gone to see her family in El Paso and was coming home. Two of my brave men died as well, defending her."

"We've all lost many."

"Yes, but I should have been on that stage so I could be with her." He blew his nose, but even looking off, the wetness in his lashes gave him away.

"No, God had some other plans for you. Look around. You are king to all these people. They live and eat well; they are not in harm's way."

"You are saying what?"

"I am saying I envy you and what you do here."

"It is expensive, so many to feed . . ." Cardin opened the liquor cabinet and took down a bottle of Kentucky whiskey.

Slocum nodded at him. "Days, weeks, even months, from now this will be over. I will wire you and tell you where she is at."

"But what will you do?" Cardin handed him the half-full tumbler.

"Ever wonder where smoke goes? One minute it is there, the next you don't know."

"What then?"

"It will be your turn to convince her who you are."

"I've never known a man quite like you. You could take her and the money she has and go to Mexico—South America."

"I'll send you the wire."

Cardin stared at him as if unsure what to say, then tossed down some of the whiskey and wiped his mouth on the back of his hand. "May God speed your journey."

"I can use his help."

14

Slocum stood against the building's adobe side and put the last of the roll-your-own to his lips. He inhaled and then blew out the final mouthful. After appraising the darkness and shadows, he looked over at the Sonoran sombrero, with the shorter wearer's back to the wall and feet set out in sandals. Ready or not, it was time to go. In a flip off his forefinger and thumb, he sent the last sparks from his cigarette out on the dirt street. With an elbow he nudged the short one beside him and spoke in Spanish. "Let's go to Isabella's. I am thirsty."

A mumble answered him and he led the way, pausing for a moment to look at the horses hipshot at the rack. His six-gun in his waistband under the serape, he reset it so it didn't gouge him so much and went through the space between the ponies to the porch.

"Hey, you got some *dinero,* ah—*mi amigo*?" A drunk staggered over with his hand out.

Slocum shook his head. The drunk blinked, then stared at Slocum's hard look in the half-light as if he had seen death—his own—and backed away. "I am sorry. I am sorry."

Ignoring him, Slocum shouldered his way though the batwing doors into the smoky interior. Men were betting on the chuck-a-luck wheel and shouting as they lost or won fistfuls of money. A black-haired woman wearing a frilly black and red dress was sprawled on top the bar with her exposed bare legs spread apart, kissing some guy with his finger poking her cunt. Several dust-floured men were around them, overseeing the action with mugs of beer in their hands, cheering the man on.

Slocum found Montoya in the back booths and let Wink slide in first. "Sorry," he mumbled to her under his breath.

Beneath the wide sombrero, she shook her head to dismiss his concern. A short barmaid came over and Slocum ordered two beers. When she was gone, he spoke to Montoya. "Where is Altovar?"

"Earlier, he paid a man two pesos to look in all the stables and wagon yards for this one. A while ago, that one came and got him. He thinks he's found the one you want, at Espinosa's Livery. He went to see if that is him."

They both looked as the woman from the bar came by riding piggyback on the finger fucker. Her shouting and screaming for him to hurry made the crowd laugh. Her bare legs flailed and kicked as he held them up and they went by the booth. Catcalls of obscenities and what to do to her filled the blue air.

"Let's go now," Slocum said and slid out. He eyed the crowd, saw no threat and let Wink go first. Halfway to the front door, a red-faced mick stepped from the bar and reached for her sleeve.

"Hey, you—"

Slocum had him by the wrist quick as a cat; ducked under it, wrenching it out of place, and then threw him at the bar. He smashed into it, spilling another's beer and causing some grumbling. Holding his arm to his side, the mick whined. "Damn yah, ah, yah broke me frigging arm."

"No, worse than that, I dislocated it. Keep your gawdamn hands to yourself from now on." The threesome went outside without another incident.

On the porch, Montoya gave a head toss and they went east.

"You all right, Chappo?" Slocum asked her as they hurried after their man, up the walk past the dark houses and stores. All the time, Slocum was looking in the shadowy night for any movement or threat.

"Whew, tough place," she hissed at him.

"It got a little raw in there tonight, even for Isabella's."

"Why did he reach for me?"

"I guess he thought you were a kid and he planned to pick on you."

"I had my hand on my gun. If you hadn't stopped him, I was going to jam it in his guts."

"You're learning,"

"Trying . . ."

"Come on. Montoya wants us," he said, seeing the man waving to him.

"What's happening?" Slocum asked the man when they reached him in front of the livery.

"He took his horse and left with a woman earlier."

"Can we find his horse? He will probably murder her."

"Altovar is coming. Maybe he will have an idea."

"Did he learn her name?"

"Señor, the livery man says he left only a short while ago with a Mexican woman," Altovar said, looking around displeased.

"Did the man know her?"

Altovar shook his head.

"If we don't find her, that woman will be dead," Wink said.

"Each of us go in a different way and ask about a man and woman with a horse. Wink, you stay with me."

"What will we do if we find him?" Montoya asked.

"Arrest him and bring him back here."

"We are not the law, señor."

"Tonight you are—he offers resistance, kill him. He is wanted for murder in several places."

They both nodded, and Montoya said, "Señor Cardin said we should help you. We will do our best."

"Be careful."

They agreed, and Montoya went east, Altovar south, and Slocum, with a head toss to Wink, headed north up the dark street. They met an old man walking with a stick.

"*Mi amigo*, a while ago, a man went up this street with a woman and a horse. I need to find him."

"No see them. No see them."

"*Gracias.*" Slocum hurried on, and a woman came to the lighted doorway of her *casa*. He removed his sombrero at the yard gate. "Señora, a man, a woman and a horse went by here a short while ago."

She stood in the doorway. "You mean that *puta*, Lupe. She is always bringing poor men home and robbing them." Then she came down from the doorway and pointed up the street. "See that second hovel across the street at the next corner. She went up there not thirty minutes ago with that poor man and his *caballo*. Bet she has already robbed him."

"*Gracias,*" he said with a head toss for Wink to follow him, and started across the street.

"Think it's him?" Wink whispered, catching up.

"We'll soon know," he said. "You cover the back. Get in a good place to cover any escape. I'll hold up till you are in place."

"It won't take me long."

"Be careful."

She was gone, and he gave her plenty of time to get set, listening to some couple verbally fighting nearby. The *jacal* had some candles lit on the inside, but thin drapes covered the windows on the street side. At last ready, he drew his Colt, went to the front door and knocked.

"Go away. I have business tonight," a woman inside said.

He knocked again, hoping she would come and open the door.

"Not tonight!"

Again he rapped on it.

"Go away, you donkey dick, I am busy."

"I'll handle him."

He wished he'd known Henny's voice.

"No—" she pleaded.

"You no-good dumb son of a bitch—" He jerked the door open. Slocum struck him over the forehead with his gun butt, jerked his gun away from him as he went down to his knees, and stood over him as the woman screamed.

Wink burst in the back door, her gun ready. "Get him?"

"Come and look," he said and turned to the howling woman. "Shut up or I'll do the same thing to you."

Wink pried the man's hand away from his face and then nodded. "He's one of them. It's Henny Williams."

"Who are you?" Henny asked, looking first at her then at Slocum.

"The woman you did not kill in Kansas," she said, the pistol still in her hand.

"Yeah, I told that dumb colonel we needed to be sure that you were dead 'cause you was the only one could testify against us. But he said they got you."

"Tell me one thing," she said, cold as ice. "Why did you cut up all those women?"

"I had to. They was whores and they would tell on me."

"Tell who?"

"My mother."

"He murdered whores?" Lupe asked, wide eyed in the flickering light.

"Lots of them," Wink said with a bob of her head, and holstered her .32.

Slocum breathed a sigh of relief at her actions and nodded his approval. "Tonight he'd have killed you, Lupe."

On her knees Lupe began to cross herself and pray in earnest to the Virgin Mary.

"Come on, Henny. They've got a cell for you." He jerked him up by the shirt collar, and with the wanted man in tow, they left Lupe to her fervent prayers.

"You won't let them hang me, will you? Will you?"

"I'd do like the French did to your kind, pull you to pieces with teams of horses."

"Oh, no. Oh, no!"

"Shut up!" Slocum said, jerking him along by the collar and turning back in time to see Wink kick him hard in the butt.

"Why do that?"

Hands on her hips, she scowled at him. "I really wanted to shoot his ass off, so that had to do."

Slocum chuckled, and soon they were both laughing, with their sullen prisoner marching ahead of them.

15

"Where will you go next?" Cardin asked.

"Wichita," Slocum said.

"Why there?"

"We can take a train to there from here. Then we can ride down in the Indian Territory easy from that point. There's been a few train robberies lately in the Nations that they say our last man on her list was in on."

"Isn't that a dangerous country?" Cardin asked.

"You can get your horses stolen while you're taking a bath," she said, and they laughed with her.

Cardin took them to the station in his carriage and shook Slocum's hand. "Very interesting to meet you. You are indeed a very different man. But I'd be damned glad to have you covering my backside in the event of trouble."

Then he swept off his hat and bowed to her. "You, my sweet lady, are a rose in a thicket of thorns. Mind that man; he has your interests in his heart."

"Thanks," she said and hugged his neck. "We thank you and your men for all their help. Kansas is sending lawmen out to take him back and stand trial. We have one more."

"What will you do after that?"

She paused. The bright sunshine shone on her tanned

face and she shook her head. "I won't know until this is over."

"If you need anything—anything—wire me. Men, money, help."

She nodded and thanked him. He held her hands out at a distance. "I lost my first wife to Apaches. I stand here today and wonder if I will ever see you again."

"Perhaps," she said and smiled for him.

Slocum tossed their saddles on the car platform and then their war bags. He assisted her on the steps of the waiting car, waved at Cardin, and they went inside the coach. In a jerk of cars, the Atchison, Topeka and Santa Fe passenger service pulled out. They found a place, and the porter helped them lug their gear to it.

Slocum tipped him a dime and he smiled. "You all sure have a good trip now."

The rock of the train, the acrid smell of coal smoke swept back in the car, the clacking of expansion cracks in the track, stopping at stations and buying food from the hawkers, back on, and each hour another twenty-five miles passed. So two and a half days later, they climbed down in the night's darkness at the Wichita depot. A black baggage man came with a handcart. "You's need a taxi?"

"Yes," Slocum said. "Cattleman's Hotel."

"I sure gets you one." Their things loaded on his cart, the man hauled their luggage around in front and began dickering with the taxi driver. He finally turned back and began loading their things in the taxi. "He takes you's dere for a dollar."

Slocum gave him two quarters for his efforts. "Thanks."

The ride to the hotel was quiet compared to his recollections of the trail drive days. All-night sessions of shooting off pistols were a simple enough part of the times; wild women running naked down the streets in races that drew many bettors out in the torchlit street. The law turned its head sideways, and the gaming went on, with more bare breasts and exposed butts on the line ready to charge off at the starter's gun. *Goddamn it, rest of you boys don't shoot this time till after the race starts.*

Slocum helped Wink off the taxi at the hotel. Inside he took a room for them and ordered up a bathtub and hot water. The desk clerk promised it would be taken care of immediately. They went upstairs and waited in the room. In a few minutes, the tub arrived, and two black youths soon packed up pails of steaming hot water for their usage. Left alone, they began to undress, numb from all the travel and the lack of any good sleep in the past two days. After they'd both bathed, they fell on the bed side by side to sleep twelve hours like logs.

"Whew," she said seated on the side of the bed, brushing her hair with long strokes. "It's good to be here, but that was a long trip."

Slocum agreed, standing at the window looking at the street below. "Trains are the quick way, but they aren't the easiest."

"What do we do next?"

"Get a meal, pick out some horses and head south."

She looked up and wet her lips. "I kinda thought we might go tomorrow."

He laughed. "Hell, the colonel can wait that long." He swept her up and kissed her hard. "I'm used to having to be somewhere. Guess we can take our own sweet time, huh?"

She swept the hair back from her face and smiled up at him. "Exactly."

"Let's find us a meal, then pick out some horses and a pack animal, then we can saunter back here." He grinned.

"Excellent."

The late breakfast in a café worked well, and they were soon out on the boardwalk headed for the livery down the street. The too bright noon sun shone down on them until they made the turn into the shaded alleyway and the pungent aroma of horse manure assailed them.

"What kin I do fur ya?" the toothless man asked, leaning on the pitchfork.

"You the man?"

"Don't look like a boy, do I?"

"No, sir. I need a couple good saddle horses."

"Well, you come to the right place. I got them all prices." The old man nodded, looking them over as if apprehending what they needed. "I got a stout bay, but he's a little too much for her. You'd like him. And for her a nice brown mare."

"I'd rather have horses."

"This mare's a handy one, but I savvy horses. Maybe there's a white-stocking-legged Barb pony she might like."

"Let's go look at them."

He set the fork aside and led the way back through the sour-smelling barn that was draped in cobwebs from the rafters under the loft floor. The old man brought the bay out of the stall and gave Slocum the lead rope. Then he trudged down the line and took a stocking-legged sorrel out ahead, into the area behind the barn where several horses were in pens.

She caught up with Slocum and gave a head toss. "Don't look too hard, but in the corral over there, isn't that the Mexican's roan that I rode down here on?"

From the corner of his eye, he saw the familiar ewe neck and face full of mane, then nodded. "That's him."

The old man opened a gate and hitched the bay to the corral fence. "Look them over. You can ride them or whatever."

"That roan horse yours?" Slocum asked.

"Nope, a fellar's boarding him here, why?"

"Couple weeks ago down in the Nation, someone stole him from her."

"Hmm, he's a gambler named Kyle Jones. You can find him down at the Emporium Saloon. Never said how he got him. He's a stout horse; I can tell looking at him."

Slocum nodded to her. "I'll go see about him later. I lost a big dun the same time."

The old man shook his head. "Not seen one of them lately."

Slocum set in to checking the two horses and decided the

stocking-legged, dish-faced horse should suit her needs. Maybe five, he appeared broke and handy. The bay acted full of fire, and by his teeth looked to be six. He had a few wire scars, but none of them appeared to hurt his movement or gait.

"How much for the pair?" Slocum asked the old man.

"Forty for the bay, and the Barb fifty."

"Sixty hard cash."

He took off his weatherbeaten hat and scratched his thin head of gray. "Can't do that."

"Sixty-five or I'll go look some more."

"Seventy. Them's good ponies."

"Didn't say they weren't. Sixty-seven and half."

The old man straightened his back and shook his head. "Sixty-eight and you're robbing me."

"If I wasn't in a hurry—I'd've bought 'em for sixty bucks."

"No way, no way."

"Get the shoes on the Barb reset. His feet are too long."

"I ain't—"

"I'll pay you. Get it done today. We're heading out early in the morning."

"Lady, I don't know where you found him, but he ain't a bad hand at seeing horses."

She thanked him and smiled as Slocum counted him out the money.

"That Jones ain't no stranger to trouble," he said, stuffing the money down his overall bib; then he snickered. "Guess you ain't either."

"I'll be wary."

Once out in front, he sent her back to the hotel with a kiss and a promise he would not be long, and then he walked the block to the Emporium. The large room was early afternoon quiet, and he stepped up to the bar and ordered a beer. A few men sat in the back of the room playing cards under lighted lamps on a wagon wheel overhead.

"Kyle Jones back there?"

"Yeah, you need him?" the bartender said and set the foaming mug down.

"I want to meet him. Which one is he?"

"The guy in the white hat."

Slocum nodded and put two dimes down, one for the beer, one for the tip. The bartender thanked him. Slocum studied the man he figured to be in his forties. Gray around the ears, thin build, with the pale complexion under black stubble of a man that didn't live outdoors.

He sauntered over and stood back, beer in his hand.

"Want to sit in, drover?" a big red-faced man asked, looking over his fresh hand.

"I ain't intruding?"

Jones looked up like it was the first time he'd seen him. Slocum knew that was a lie—the man had watched his every move since he came in the place. "Have a chair."

"Thanks."

"Five card draw," the big man on his right said, folding. "Earl Sandwich is my name."

"Tom White's mine."

"I've seen you before," Jones said.

"I guess. I was here a couple years ago with a herd."

"No, not here, somewhere's else. I'll think of it."

"Been lots of places," Slocum said and put some money on the table in front of himself.

The next hand, the quiet man across from him, called Neal, dealt. He was behind a full beard and mustache that sprouted out in three directions, and the cards came to Slocum. Two treys, a jack, a six and an eight.

Jones bid two dollars and Neal folded. Sandwich stayed in and drew three cards. Slocum did the same and drew three—no help. Pair of threes was not a big hand, but he watched Jones take one card. Did the gambler have two pair or was he trying to fill in a straight or flush?

Jones bid two dollars, Sandwich folded, and Slocum called him.

His eyes shifted and he looked over at Slocum. "What you got?"

"I paid to see yours."

"Guess you can—ace high." He spilled the cards out.

"Pair of treys."

Jones leaned back in his chair and folded his arms. "Why have I got this idea you ain't a drover?"

"That was your assumption."

"We playing cards or jawing?" Sandwich asked.

"What is your business in Wichita?" Jones put both hands on the table.

"I'm looking for a buckskin and a roan that were stolen off me a few weeks back."

He frowned at Slocum. "Roan horse?"

"Yes, the one that's down in the stables."

"I bought him."

"Good, get out the papers."

"They're in my room."

"No problem. I've got all day."

"Listen—you accusing me—"

"I ain't accusing anyone. That horse and the Mexican saddle were property of my wife's."

"Mexican saddle?"

"The one with the silver on it."

"I've seen you riding it," Sandwich said.

"Don't anyone move." Jones had a derringer in his hand and waved it at the three of them as he rose and started to back away. "Anyone follows me out of here is a dead sumbitch. That goes for you especially, White."

"I'll keep that in mind," Slocum said.

Jones backed across the room holding the gun steady on them. Then he turned and fled out the batwing doors.

"That worthless outfit," Sandwich said as he rose and frowned, looking over at Slocum. "What the hell're you going to do? He's gone for that horse."

"Borrow that shotgun he keeps under the bar, walk down there and give him a chance to surrender."

"What if he don't?"

"Guess he'll need to have a tombstone picked out."

"Clancy, give him your shotgun and loaded too," Sandwich called out. "Why, that no-good outfit. You reckon he's the one stole it in the first place?"

Slocum shook his head. "But I think he knew it was stolen, which is just as bad."

"Amen. I hate a damn thief, especially a hoss thief."

Slocum took the sawed-off shotgun from Clancy, broke it open and inserted two high-brass shells. "Thanks. I won't be long."

"Probably won't need it for days. It's got a hair trigger."

Slocum nodded and headed for the batwing doors. If there was a way, he'd stop him. His boot heels strode the hollow-sounding boardwalk, holding the scattergun in both hands and drawing the shocked looks of several women on the way. He nodded politely to them and continued toward the sign marked "LIVERY."

In the alleyway of the barn, he could see Jones out back, busy saddling the roan. Slocum continued through the horse-piss-smelling barn until Jones whirled. Seeing Slocum, he started leading the horse away, but then gave up and ducked behind the corral, leaving the roan in Slocum's way. On the run, he dodged a gelding and Jones was out of sight, but a shot from the side of an outhouse across the alley gave away his position.

Determined to either take him in custody or send him to hell, Slocum kept coming, hoping the gambler would expose himself. He used the corral for cover as long as he dared, then broke for the last place the man had shot from. Reaching the outhouse, he went to the left of it, thinking Jones might have a gun trained on the right side.

He caught sight of Jones at the back of a store, arm extended and pointing to the right.

"Drop the gun!"

Jones whirled, gun in hand, and took the right-hand barrel of the shotgun's blast in the chest. The revolver rolled forward then dropped from his fingers and his knees buckled. Slocum walked across the yard and looked at the blood on his white shirt.

"Who sold you that roan?" He gazed at him as the man tried to get up.

"I'm . . . dying . . ."

"Who sold you the horse?"

"Get a doctor . . ."

"When you tell me who sold you that horse."

"Yates . . . Cy . . . Yates . . ." His eyes went blank.

"What's going on here?" a frock-coated lawman demanded, out of breath from running.

"Man stole my horse."

"You ain't got any right to shoot up the town. This is not the damn cow town days, Mr. . . ."

"Tom White, Fort Worth, Texas."

"Buck Davenport, assistant town marshal, and my boss Ollie Acres ain't going to like this shooting business—no sir, not one bit."

"Better have an undertaker pick him up." Slocum motioned to the dead man. "My roan horse is loose and may run off. I'm staying at the Cattleman's Hotel."

"Where you going with that shotgun? We have a gun—"

"I know. That's why I had to borrow it from Clancy at the Emporium. He wants it back."

"There will be a hearing over this . . . ah, White."

Slocum nodded that he had heard the man, and leading the roan in one hand, gun in the other, he headed for the livery. *Who the hell was Cy Yates?*

16

Slocum stood by the window and looked at the street traffic. "Wish I knew who Cy Yates was."

"I never heard of him. Hadn't we better get down in the Nation before some Kansas lawman learns who you are?" she asked, pulling on her canvas pants and then standing up to tuck in her shirt, button the fly and put up the suspenders.

"Not a bad idea. We better wait till dark. Then we can outmaneuver the law. Broad daylight, they might see us."

She agreed. "You stay here and I'll go see about having the horses ready, so they don't see you. Can we trust the stables man?"

"I think so. Sell him back the Barb. Price is no issue. We won't need him with the roan back."

"Good. I can do that and not draw much attention."

"Hmm." He slipped up behind her and ran his hand over her butt. "You better go out the back way; every loafer in town may be ogling this."

She blushed and nodded. "I guess I don't care anymore how it looks, I kinda like wearing pants. Beats riding a horse in a skirt."

"Looks good too. Be careful." He kissed her and twisted her around until her ripe figure was pressed to him.

She came up for air in his arms. "Whew, I better go or we'll be in the bed again."

They both laughed.

Wink headed for the stables, and he stretched out on the bed to read the newspaper:

> The Missouri Western passenger train was held up at gunpoint by members of the vicious Bowdry Gang, Monday at noon, Towbridge Station. The outlaws are headed by Colonel Charles Bowdry, a former Confederate officer. Several former members of the Jesse James Gang are also aligned with Bowdry according to rumors.
>
> At 12:15 pm Central Standard Time, Thursday, September 30, the gang of eight commandeered the express car of the Number Twenty-Seven passenger train at the Towbridge Station, wounding two Wells Fargo guards and dynamiting the safe. No passengers were injured in the incident. The safe contents included five thousand in cash and a thousand in silver dollars that the gang scattered all over in their escape. Sheriff Buck Davenport said it was the most lucrative tracking any posse ever did. But the gang split near the Grand River and no further money could be located.
>
> Wells Fargo has offered a five hundred dollar reward for Bowdry dead or alive and two-fifty apiece for his henchmen in like condition.
>
> This robbery and other similar criminal acts are certainly removing the Indian Territory from any congressional consideration of statehood. On the floor of the U.S. House of Representatives, Missouri

Congressman Hack Thorton has called for a full congressional appraisal of the federal law enforcement issue in the Indian Territory. Thorton claims his constituents in southwest Missouri live under the threat of the violent lawlessness that spills over his state's border.

Perhaps the congressman does not realize that Missouri spawned Jesse James and his infamous gang. When more reports are available, our reporter in the field, Mark Allen, who is currently investigating the illegal liquor trade in the Nations, will forward them.

Slocum rose and went to the open window. The red orange rays of sundown speared the smudged glass on the upper half. Through the open half he could see the traffic and the gentle wind fluttering clothing and some dust. Summer was starting to pass, with the intense heat letting up. His mind was still on wintering in San Antonio—he could almost hear the soft guitars' music, and see a dark-eyed señorita beating time on castanets. Her defiant dark eyes flashing, she held the castanets high, her olive arms intertwining above her head as she stomped to the music.

A key clicked in the lock and he glanced at the door. Her fresh face shone as she slipped in. He turned back to study the buggies and rigs moving down the street. "Any problem?"

"I don't think so. He paid me twenty-five for the Barb. Ours will be ready when we are."

"We'll wait until twilight is about over before we ease out of here. Your man's robbed a train this week in the Nation." He indicated the paper on the bed.

"Bowdry?"

"Yes. They say there's eight men in the gang. Some members of the old James gang."

"We may need help."

He agreed and took her in his arms and hugged her. "We may."

"We going to Hurricane's?"

"Yes, I figure we can headquarter there as easy as any place."

She looked up at him. "Fine. I'm no longer afraid of medicine men, and I like him and Blue."

"It'll take two days, if we don't have our horses stolen."

"We better not let that happen."

He checked the sun's fast disappearing light, then gave her a squeeze and let her go. "We'll go out the back way in ten minutes. Grab your things."

They eased out the rear door of the Cattleman's Hotel and shared the alley with yowling tomcats on the make. A screaming female went whizzing by them with her mounted lover attached, humping away.

"She doesn't like it," Slocum said, amused, carrying both canvas bags.

"And from the looks of things, he may not be the first one she's had to endure tonight," she said and shook her head. Slocum laughed and directed her around a rig parked behind a store. "You may be right; there are plenty of suitors."

He checked the girths and then boosted her up on the roan. She had the lead to the roan and the brown pack horse. With the headstall in his left hand, he checked the bay horse, holding his head close to his leg while he mounted—in case. A boot toe in each stirrup, he let go. The big horse walked carefully as they went out the alley headed for the ferry over the Arkansas.

His coaxing and chastising needed to work. Last thing he needed was a buck off or the horse crashing into something in the gathering darkness. "Damn you, get that out of your head."

She laughed softly at his plight. "He really wants to buck, doesn't he?"

"He'll get better," he promised her, checking him close with the reins.

The sleepy ferryman took their money—ten cents apiece for horses and people. Then he began winding the windlass that powered them over. When they were halfway across, Slocum looked back at the twinkling lights of town. He held the bay and the roan by the bridles—they acted the most upset by the hollow-sounding barge underneath their hooves.

Wichita had come a long ways since the railhead days when they drove cattle up there less than five years earlier. It had been wide open, rip-snorting wild—the guns went off all night and the music never stopped until the ragtime kid fell off the stool stone drunk. One night, full of rotgut whiskey, Billy Muggs rode his Ten Bears horse into the Buffalo Wallow Saloon and put him on the pool table. Caused a helluva fight with the owner, who disliked the horse poop on his velvet. The Williams Brothers, Marl and Matt, who owned the cattle outfit, would have rather fought than danced with good-looking women. If they couldn't find a fight, they went to fists with each other. So one little Irish saloon keeper and his two goons were just like having eggs on toast for them.

Slocum recalled a young black girl called herself Lucy, came out to their campgrounds the first night they reached the area. Maybe fourteen or fifteen years old, a slip of a thing who wore a shabby dress that only came to her knees.

"You's guys come all the way up cheer from Texas?" she asked, looking them over in the twilight.

"We sure did. Have a seat," Muscle Monroe said and patted a place beside him.

"Reckon you boss, he don't mind?" She looked around kind of wary.

"Hell, no. Take a seat, we need to talk."

She dropped on the ground and hugged her knees. It was no problem for those across the fire from her to see the thin mahogany legs, her bare butt and all else. Made Phil Day's eyes bug out and he liked to choke on his last bite. It was the first pussy he'd ever seen, he confided later.

Cookie found her a plate of food and she ate in her lap,

bony knees and most of her dark crossed legs exposed. The white bare soles shone in the night.

She knew them boys had been on the trail for months getting up on their knees to roll over at night. Using her fork to punctuate the firelight, she said, "I's charge a dime apiece for a good long toss in the hay and don't give no credit."

A moan went up. "No credit?"

"No credit, that's be my way. But you's boys ever get your big poker in some black stuff, you's won't never want the white kind again." Then she threw her hands over her mouth as if to hide behind them.

There was a pooling of the resources and cards drawn for each of "you's" turn. High card was first. Slocum drew a queen and was third.

On her back, Lucy laughed the whole time she entertained them. She'd shout, "My, my, you's done got the biggest pecker I's ever had in me." She told them all that. Then when they got to pounding her ass hard, she'd huff and puff like they were really getting it on with her. In the end, she went skipping off in the dark prairie, singing and seeming none the worse for the wear, over a dollar richer—miracle too, none of the crew caught the clap from her.

Ah, Wichita, she'd never be the same. All that innocence lost that night in a black girl's snatch on the south side of the Arkansas. Several of his saddle mates would never be boys again; they rode back to Texas as men. Their rite of passage after three tough months on the trail really was completed screwing a dark-skinned whore close to their own age, on the ground.

Slocum led the high-headed horses off the ferry in the lantern light. He held the roan until Wink was on board, then gave her the leads.

"Kinda silly to me for you two to take off at night," the ferryman complained and spat tobacco. "Man might break his neck getting throwed."

"I'll keep that in mind," Slocum said as he checked the bay and swung on him.

"I wasn't near as worried about you as much as I was about the pretty lady."

"I'll take that under advisement."

"Don't reckon you will."

"Why's that?"

"'Cause you don't give a damn about what I think anyway." The man hung on his overall suspenders in the lantern light and nodded with a solemn look.

"You know—" Slocum checked the circling bay up short. "You just may be right." A head toss to her, and they went off in the starlight.

It was still two days' hard ride to Hurricane's outfit.

17

Floured in trail dust, they slipped off the last long hill riding through the tall bluestem stalks tossed by the wind. The buildings and corrals in sight, Slocum put his hands on his hips and stretched his stiff back. Their horses from time to time dropped their heads down and snorted with the weariness of the hard push, obvious even in the stout bay.

"Reckon he's home?" she asked.

"I don't care. I could sleep two days and these ponies need some rest too."

"A bath might be nice."

He twisted in the saddle. "Might hit the spot if I don't fall asleep first."

She stretched her arms over her head and smiled at him. "It's been a hard trip down here all right—but guess I'm getting in shape."

He narrowed his eyes and looked at her. Then he chuckled and at last shook his head. "You've done wonderful, girl."

"I keep thinking how I'll ever go back to being a housewife when this is over."

"Aw, something will turn up."

"You mean Ralph Cardin?"

"Hey, I'm not shoving you off on anyone. The man is infatuated with you. He's well-to-do and has a lovely ranch out there. I think you could live on your own terms with him."

"Such as?"

"Wear pants when you wanted. Forget a bustle and corset and be yourself with him."

She nodded. "But you have not left yet."

"I don't know when I'll have to leave."

"Don't tell me—" She tossed her hair back as if to clear her head. "And don't figure on sleeping much till you go. I'm spoiled."

"Deal," he said, setting the bay in a jog for Hurricane's.

It was a thirty-pound, lank shoat that ran out of hiding and shot underneath the bay like a bullet. Too much for the bay gelding; he went plunging across the yard, grunting like a boar with every effort. Slocum lost a stirrup; then he gave it up and dove off to the right.

On the ground laughing, he watched her charge after the bay to catch him. With a wince or two, he found his feet and started to meet her as she led him back. Lucky thing Blue and Hurricane weren't home—he'd have never heard the end of it.

He took the reins and caught the headstall. The gelding blew roller out his nose and fell backward. Slocum hung on, keeping up until he quieted down, talking softly all the time.

"You aren't going to try to ride him?" She looked shocked.

"I don't want him getting in the habit of doing things like this." In the saddle, he released the bridle and checked the horse. The bay short loped in a circle and tried nothing— perfect acting, like all the buck was gone.

"Wonder where they went."

"Getting to be the cool time of the year; they always have get powwows then. Probably went to some stomp."

"I'll go rustle up some food. You draw some water we can heat for a bath."

"Ugh, you want me to do squaw work?"

She gave him a shove with her elbow. "Yes, you need to get in shape."

"I have that coming?"

"Yes, you do," she said, piling her saddle on the ground.

"I still have you in shape to go after Bowdry."

"Yes, but will we need more help to do that?"

"I hope not. Too many men will put him on guard when the word gets out."

"But he has a new gang?"

"Just riffraff he collected. There's million like those in the Nations."

She looked at the sky for celestial help. "Whatever you think."

They were bathing in the tub when the sounds of a wagon coming down the road sent them to hopping around to dry off and get dressed.

"Must be them," she said, buttoning the front of her shirt.

"Or we got company," he said, pulling on his right boot. "One thing I hate is having a leisure bath disturbed."

She laughed. "Oh, yes, you are so formal."

"So formal. Where is my butler?"

"He quit," she said, putting up her suspenders. "It ain't Hurricane."

He nodded, strapped on his holster and headed for the front of the cabin wondering who had arrived.

"Hello," the older Indian man said, frowning at him and pausing to get down.

"Welcome. We are friends of Hurricane. He must be gone."

The man nodded that he understood and climbed off. Then he helped the woman off the seat. She, like him, was small, but she had a wide smile and once had been a very attractive woman.

"We came to do his chores. He and Blue went to Tahlequah on business. He'll be back in a few days."

"Have you had supper?"

The woman said, "No, but we will later." She set out with a bucket to milk the cow.

"I'm going to feed the pigs," he announced. "My name is Charlie. Hers is Dora."

"She's Wink, I'm Slocum."

"Glad to meet you. He went to Choteau with you, didn't he?"

"Yes."

Charlie shook his head as if impressed. "That damn Black Hawk thought no bullet could kill him."

"You know him?"

"I met him once."

"He's dead now."

"Bet there are lots of people went out and got drunk over that."

"What's Hurricane in Tahlequah about?"

"Try to heal a sick friend. Doctors can't help him."

"We may be around here for several days."

"We come morning and night to milk, gather eggs and feed the pigs," he said and threw out a pail full of whole corn on a wide fan for the squealing pigs.

"You know anything about the Bowdry Gang?"

"I know Joe Two-hearts lives on the Barren Fork River. He rides with him now."

"Can you draw me a map on how to get there?"

"Sure, but he's a mean sumbitch—" Charlie shook his head. "Maybe mean as Black Hawk." He went down on his knee and used a stick to scratch the ground, showing Slocum the roads to take and where the outlaw lived.

"They have horse races on Sunday at Barren Fork," Charlie said. "You could go there then. Lots of whites come over the line from Arkansas for them, and maybe then he won't be suspicious about you being there."

"You think Bowdry might be there?"

Charlie shook his head. "I never knew him except in the news. Booky James is another one rides for him. He's fat and usually drunk."

"Maybe he's the James Gang member they talk about."

With a loud chuckle, Charlie slapped his leg. "He never rode with Jesse James. One time he passed out at a stomp. He was lying on the ground. Must have been pissing when he went out, 'cause his pants were open. Next morning, a fighting rooster jumped on him and pecked his dick—thought it was a worm. Booky woke up screaming."

Both of them laughed.

"You know any others in the gang?"

Charlie shook his head. "I don't like his kind. Bowdry is a user of men. He never pays them much, and they soon learn they take all the risks, but that kind likes to brag—'I was in his gang.' "

Slocum agreed.

Dora and Wink returned with a half pail of milk and a small woven oak basket of brown eggs. "You ready to go, Charlie?" Dora asked him.

"I better, or I won't get to eat, huh?"

"Better," Slocum agreed and shook his slender hand. "Drive careful."

"Oh, we will or break the eggs," Charlie said and untied the reins. "See you two again."

"Where next?" Wink asked, hugging on his arm as they watched the couple drive away.

"Barren Fork. Horse races on Sunday. Bowdry may be there."

"What about Hurricane?"

"We'll look him up on the way. I'd like to have him point out these gang members Charlie named."

"Let's go to bed." She looked up from hugging him in front.

"You tired?"

She wrinkled her nose at him. "I plan to be after we get through."

He laughed. "All right, I get the idea."

She punched him in the muscle-corded belly. "You've had it all the time."

*   *   *

A rooster woke them up. He went to the doorway and let the cool wind sweep over his nakedness. Fall would soon be there. The horses were grazing down the meadow. She hugged him from behind; her rock-hard nipples stabbed his back, and her warm breath bathed his neck.

"I wish we could stay here forever."

"You tired of this business?"

"No, I still want Bowdry in jail or dead."

"Fine. We better set out for Tahlequah and find Hurricane."

"You are a taskmaster. I saved some eggs last night for us, and I have some bread left over. You saddle the horses and I'll fix breakfast."

"Yes, ma'am." He spun around and caught her by the waist, hoisting her onto the bed, Then he came between her legs, cupped her face in his hands and began to kiss her. His feet on the dirt floor, he stood on his toes and reached underneath to insert his growing erection in her.

His hips ached to pound her, and his hard pecker soon filled her snatch. He sped up his operation, and her heels began to beat a tattoo on his back as she hunched her butt at him for more and more. The world moved farther and farther away, until their breath raged from their throats and their need strained harder and harder. Then, his hands clutching both sides of her butt, he pushed off his cramping toes for the final shot and fired a volley of rounds that left him depleted.

In a mop of reddish curls, she shook her head in defeat. "Oh, my God, I may never walk again."

"Good. I'll carry you."

"To bed?" She gave him a sheepish grin.

"Wherever," he said, pulling on his pants

She scooted off the bed. "Off to Tahlequah, huh?"

"If we don't get distracted."

She stepped into her britches. "I like distractions."

"Good, but we only have two days to get down there. We better hurry."

"I will—where were we? Oh, you're saddling, I'm cooking."

His boots on, he stomped his feet in them. "I'll grain them too."

"Horses haven't had much rest."

"They'll be fine. We'll start graining them more."

In an hour, they ate breakfast, loaded the pack horse, and headed south. Some dark clouds were gathering in the northwest—a cold front coming; they'd need slickers. Mid-morning, he bought two at a general store and came out in time for the first drops. They shrugged the waxed canvas dusters on and he swung into the saddle. Rain or not, they needed to keep pushing.

His sodden hat made a gutter for rain to run off, and a chill was on his skin under his clothing. With a wrinkled finger, he pointed to a wagon yard that appeared out of the darkness and the driving rain that swept the land. She nodded in approval.

At last in the office, with the heat of the wood stove on his face, he hugged her while he waited for the man to limp to his desk.

He looked them over and shook his head. "Damndest rain I've seen in years."

"Damndest," Slocum agreed and shivered.

18

The incessant rain delayed them more. Swollen streams defied crossing, so they reached Tahlequah later, and finding Hurricane proved harder than Slocum had expected. He was nearby, on the dying man's farm. Blue rushed out and hugged Wink when they rode up.

"You been a while coming," Hurricane said.

"It's been raining where I've been."

"Been raining here too." Hurricane shook his head.

"Charlie thought Bowdry might be at Barren Fork for the Sunday races."

"Lots of people go there."

"I wanted to be here yesterday, but no way with all the damn rain we've been in. How is the friend?"

"Weak."

"Will he live?"

"If he wants to."

"I see. Now I need to find a place for us to sleep so we can start early in the morning."

"There is a schoolhouse we can use tonight. It is down the road. There is no school there now."

"Good. We have some food I bought in town, and this rain isn't over." He frowned at the growing clouds.

"It may rain more. You have found the other one?"

"Yes, Henny is in jail in Kansas by now."

Hurricane nodded. "Bowdry may be at the races."

Saturday morning brought a fresh round of showers. Slocum saddled the horses and then helped hitch the team; they left in a short while, swept by the cold wind and more rain. Hurricane knew a man named Carter he trusted who lived on the Barren Fork, and they reached his place in late afternoon.

John Carter was a tall Cherokee, a man near Slocum's height and size. He welcomed them and complained that his wife had left him for the third time, but they were welcome, especially the women, who he said could use his cookstove.

The three men sat on wooden kitchen chairs before his rock fireplace, facing the heat radiating from the crackling oak firewood and discussing Bowdry and his gang.

"Bowdry was here a few weeks ago," Carter said. "You know some of the people like him, they fought for the Confederacy."

"I did too," Slocum said. "But that's over. Bowdry killed her husband and son." He motioned to Wink, who was busy helping Blue fix the food.

Carter nodded and glanced back to where the two women worked at the stove and dry sink. "Bad deal. She's sure some good-looking woman."

"Where will Bowdry stay?"

"Maybe Joe Two-hearts's."

"How far is his place from here?" Slocum asked.

Carter shrugged. "Maybe three miles downstream."

"I'd like to see if he was there."

"Might be a good time," Carter said. "They are liable to be like us—all denned up." They laughed.

"Where's your wife?" Hurricane asked.

Carter made a face. "I think she has a new lover."

"Who?"

"Some damn boy named Pete."

Hurricane shook his head.

"I know, I know, there are more women in this world. I like her too much to give up."

"Your problem. After we eat, let's go down there," Hurricane said.

Carter looked hard into the licking flames. "Better take our guns. Two-hearts might kill us if he knows our business."

At the side of the room, Slocum explained his plans to Wink, promising to come back for her if he learned anything.

"You be careful."

"Always."

When the rain didn't deluge them, everything dripped. The hardwood trees they rode underneath, which were still short of turning into their fall foliage, proved a source of more moisture. They kept to cover, and soon Carter showed them a place to leave their horses. They hitched them to some trees and followed the big man through the wet brush down the steep hillside.

Through all the foliage, Slocum caught sight of some smoke coming from a chimney. They skirted the place in the woods and finally sought cover and a dry place in a large hay shed. Grateful to be out of the wind, they stood hunched up in the sweet-smelling interior.

"You reckon he's in the house?" Hurricane asked.

Carter shrugged. "If it was dark—someone's coming out here."

"We'll grab him and make him tell us," Hurricane said.

"Might spook them," Slocum said. "Let's hide."

They stepped back in a tie stall and heard the door creak open. Through a crack, Slocum watched the man take a pitchfork and fill it with hay. He tossed it out a side window to some horse stock in the corrals outside and put the fork back before he left for the house.

"I don't think Bowdry's here," Slocum said, checking the horses in the lot. "There isn't one in that bunch that Bowdry would even ride."

"Maybe he'll come in during the night," Carter said.

"Maybe. Who was the hay feeder?" Slocum asked.

"Some guy named Hembree—he ain't a gang member. He works for Two-hearts."

"We can check at the races; he may be there," Hurricane said, and they agreed. Slipping out, they worked their way back up the forested hill to their animals and rode back.

"Was he there?" Wink asked later that evening when they were alone.

"We don't think so. Wasn't a horse there fancy enough for him to ride."

She nodded. "I can recall that day he rode up. He did come on a sleek black Morgan horse, head high and him wearing kid gloves."

"Nothing like that at Two-hearts's today, so rather than spook them we left. Hurricane thinks he may be at the races tomorrow."

She buried her face in his chest and hugged him. "Bad as I want him, I don't want this dream to end."

He nodded and looked off into the night as he held her. *To end.* He didn't relish that either; he'd for certain miss her ripe body and unquenchable eagerness for making love.

The next morning, broken clouds drifted over, and the two women took the wagon loaded with food for the day at the races. No sign of Carter's runaway wife—Hurricane had mentioned that she might be at the races with her new lover. Then he chuckled and shook his head. "Plenty good pretty women out there—why Carter don't find new one is beyond me."

The river bottom fields, wedged in by some two-hundred-foot-tall bluffs, were jammed with parked wagons, canvas shelters, tents, crude brush arbors and camp smoke that swirled around the skirts of the women busy cooking. Screaming children played chase in and out of the rest. Old family members, wrapped in blankets, sat on chairs and rockers brought from home, and stared as if looking to find something from the past they recognized.

Naked teenage boys, despite the cool morning air, rode sleek prancing ponies around the camp bareback, showing off for the teenage girls who giggled and snuck longing looks after them in passing. Then rushed over to another friend to say how he'd noticed her—she was certain too.

Slocum did see several white men there with shiny fast horses tied to their wagons. Some nodded to him, others never saw him. For certain, they were not wasting their animals' energy in child's play. A few white women cooked on fires as well. They camped in knots and were standoffish from the free style of their hosts. Even the children stayed close to their base like tethered dogs. As if they might be in harm's way should they run about and have as much fun as the Indian young'uns were having at play.

"No sign of him," Hurricane said, twisting in the saddle and looking over things as they rode on through the encampment.

"I have not seen Two-hearts here either," Carter said.

Slocum agreed as the three of them trailed the wagon Blue drove. The colonel should stand out in this place. Maybe he wouldn't show. No telling. Carter showed them a place to set up camp.

The men helped unhitch the team and get things unloaded, and when the canvas shade was put up, Carter went off.

Hurricane shook his head. "Gone to look for that dumb woman of his. I think she runs off to get attention."

Blue looked up from her fire starting and made a face of disgust. "She's too dumb to do anything makes good sense."

"When do the races start?" Wink asked, busy making coffee grounds in a hand grinder.

"Oh, later." Hurricane shrugged. "This is not like a white man's deal where it all happens at such a time; this happens when it does—Indian time."

She smiled back at him. "I think I understand."

"When the betting fever gets hot, then they really do lots of racing and lose lots of money."

Blue made a scowl. "Some people go home naked. They even bet the clothes on their back."

"That's how they came into this world; what's so bad about going home like that?" Hurricane asked.

"Who wants to see an old man or woman staggering around naked and drunk as a hoot?"

"I don't look," Hurricane said to her and gave a head toss to Slocum. "We better go look for this colonel."

"Oh, you look—you look too much," Blue said after him.

"Keep an eye out," Slocum said to Wink. "I doubt he will recognize you in those clothes, but you two be on guard."

"We will," Wink promised, and Blue agreed with a nod, her fire at last started.

They left their horses saddled and hitched to the side of the wagon in the event they needed them, and set out on foot. Hurricane knew many and spoke to them in passing.

They reached a cluster of men squatted on the ground, and Hurricane nodded that they'd join them. Dropped down to his haunches, Slocum nodded to the few who looked his way.

". . . Benny's gray is fast—but Chookie has a fast sorrel."

"Never beat the gray . . ."

He listened to the back-and-forth conversation, until a rider going by caught his eye.

"Two-hearts," Hurricane said under his breath, never looking at him.

Well, part of Bowdry's gang was there. All he needed was for the big man to arrive. He turned his attention back to the racing business.

"I want to bet two dollars on the gray," Hurricane said. "What are you going to bet?" he asked Slocum.

"Oh, two."

Hurricane held out his hand for the money. When Slocum rose and dug it out, Hurricane put it with his and gave it to an older man. "You take care of it."

"That gray will win," the old man said and grinned, exposing a missing tooth.

The two of them began to walk down to the river. Several horses were being watered along the clear running water. Not much of a river at this point and time of year, but it looked as pure as if from melted snow. Temperature was still too cool for the children to swim in the deep hole under the sycamore with the rope tied to a limb out over it.

"Wonder if Two-hearts is making sure it is all right for him to ride in?"

"Could be," Hurricane agreed.

"I wonder where he went back there."

"No telling. He will soon be full of firewater and be bragging."

"I'd like to hear him."

"Sure. He don't know you—" Hurricane pulled on his sleeve and with a head toss indicated three riders going by at a trot.

In the center of the two Indians, on a stout horse, was the man himself. Like someone had driven a ramrod up his ass, he rode square-shouldered and chest out. Several years of military school and a vain mind combined to make the man's character. Wearing a snowy new Boss of the Plains Stetson and tailored suit, with his pants tucked in high-top black riding boots, he looked very important. Slocum knew his kind. To the Colonel Bowdrys in this world, anyone else was inferior.

"Who's with Bowdry?" Slocum asked.

"Gang members, I guess."

"I better get back to camp. She catches sight of him, she may start shooting." He took off running through the loose sand on the slope. He didn't want anything to happen to her—she'd be no match for three of them. No telling what she might do—no telling.

With them in sight, he hurried off to the side so he might not be noticed, crossing wagon tongues and through camps, keeping the white hat in his vision as it bobbed above things to his right on the road. Slocum apologized to a few where he cut through their camp and hurried on.

Then he stopped beside a weather gray tailgate piled with harness. Bowdry was going to stop and talk to the camp of white men he'd observed earlier. Might be other gang members there too. No telling. This large camp was no place to have a shoot-out; stray bullets might find the innocent. But he needed to know more about Bowdry—where he was staying to start with. Damn, he'd give a lot to hear what he was saying to those men.

So close to having him in his hands and yet so far away. Still, if he could keep track of him, he might have a chance to separate him from the others. From what he could see they were putting his horse with theirs on a picket rope. Slocum rubbed his palms on the top of his legs—he needed a good plan. At the moment nothing looked too feasible.

"What's he doing?" Hurricane asked, joining him.

"Jabbering with those white men we passed coming in here."

"I think I saw a Light Horseman."

"Who are they?"

"Cherokee National Police. It just may be one, but I think they are here looking for them."

"Will they move in and arrest them?"

"Maybe, if the marshals from Fort Smith are here too."

"I don't know many of them."

"I got more bad news for you." Hurricane said. "Those two damn brothers from Fort Scott are here. I seen the big Ap horse."

The two deputies from Fort Scott. The Abbott brothers. "I better take a hike—damn, I was so sure we could separate him from his men and take him back to Kansas to hang."

Hurricane gave him a shove on the shoulders. "We better get you back to your horse."

Slocum nodded in disgust, and they went wide of the camp where the colonel was at.

"What's wrong?" Wink asked when they returned.

He shook his head. "I have to leave—"

"Leave?" She blinked at him in disbelief.

"Leave."

She closed her eyes tight shut and shook her head. "But why?"

"I told you—" He tightened the cinch. "Don't have time to talk about it. Promise me you won't do anything stupid like try to shoot Bowdry. The law is here and we think they'll take him."

"But . . . but . . ."

His bedroll tied on behind the cantle, he turned and kissed her—not hard. He felt like he'd been kicked in the gut; leaving her wasn't going to be easy. How did they ever track him there? He looked down in her sad eyes. "Promise me no gunplay."

"Promise."

He shook Hurricane's hand and hugged Blue's shoulder, whispering thanks in her ear.

"Take this medicine," Hurricane said and handed him a small pouch. "Maybe it will protect you as you ride."

Slocum nodded, put his foot in the stirrup and looked at the gap in the bluffs. "That a way to the top?" He indicated with a head toss to Hurricane.

"Tough trail, but you can get on top."

"All I need."

"Come again when you can stay longer." Hurricane smiled and hugged Wink's shoulders as she sniffed in a kerchief.

Slocum didn't look back. He booted the bay for the gap— needed some space between him and the Abbott brothers.

A few minutes later, he was scrambling on foot over the broken rocks, leading the bay and following the narrow trail that led straight to the blue sky overhead. Out of breath at the top, he wiped his sweaty face on his sleeve. No sign of pursuit, and he could still hear the noisy shouting in the camp when he swung a leg over and set out in a long trot for the northeast.

19

Not taking the roads, he rode used game trails and moved through the sweeping tall bluestem. Coming over a high rise, he paused at a log cabin in late afternoon, and a short young Indian woman came to the doorway and hushed her barking black dog. Her dress had seen better days, and two bashful children hid in her skirts. High cheekbones, her complexion was dark; brown lips set in a line, and her black eyes questioned him.

"I need to water my horse."

She nodded and motioned to the rock-cement tank. "Help yourself."

"I'd also like buy some food," he said and dismounted.

"I could make some fry bread."

"That would be fine. I'll water him."

"It will be a little while."

"I am in no hurry." *Now.* He undid the girth and led the tired bay down the path to the tank. A check of the ridge and he saw nothing, but the wind shifting grass. Be great cattle country—a man could marry an Indian woman and live on this land. A man not wanted by the law, who could stay in one place.

The bay eagerly slurped up great drafts of the tank's clear

contents. Slocum drank his fill from the end of the rusty pipe bringing water out of the spring and spilling it into the trough. The cool liquid was refreshing. Then he washed his face with his kerchief and wrung it out, feeling the wind dry his wet skin. Good to just relax for a few moments.

He hunched his stiff shoulder muscles and sat on the edge of the tank to rest while he waited for her food. From there he'd planned to swing west. In a few days, he'd be at Council Oaks and could head south for San Antonio on the old Chisholm Trail.

When she called him into her small cabin to eat, she informed him her name was Bee. That her children's names were Kind and He-too, the boy. They sat on a bench at the side and swung their legs like most children in confinement. When Slocum looked over at them, the girl giggled and then tried to hide her face in her fists. The boy, a year younger, remained stone-faced, as if nothing bothered him.

"They see few strangers," she said, pouring him coffee. "No cream—no sugar."

"Fine," he said, understanding that she was apologizing for not having any. "I like it black."

Her fry bread was filled with red beans and drew the saliva to his mouth. The flavoring was good and he nodded in approval. Seated at the wooden table opposite her, he didn't look around, for fear he might make her feel inferior because of the room's bareness.

"You wish more?" she asked, when he finished the first piece.

He shook his head, fearing that that was to be the children's meal. He raised the cup up and heard the dog barking—someone was coming.

"Take the children and go hide; there may be bad ones coming here." He set down the stained mug and drew his Colt. At the doorway, he looked back and saw her herding them out the back way. She gave him a scared look and then ran out after them. No sign of the intruders, but he could hear them coming off the ridge and he hushed the dog. No time to run. It wasn't the Abbott brothers, more like a gang or a posse. Maybe he'd stirred up a hornet's nest going after the colonel.

"He's down there," an unfamiliar voice shouted. "See his horse."

He stepped out and could see a half dozen riders and the big black horse of Bowdry's charging downhill. Damn, all he had was a pistol. A good rifle would have been handy.

Two shots from the bunch, and he took cover at the side of the cabin. Using a notched log for stability, he aimed and took down a horse that went end-over-end and landed on his rider, who never made a sound—that left six. And they drew up in shock.

"Slocum, you sumbitch, we've got you cornered, better give up now!" Bowdry shouted. "Go around, boys." He waved for his men to scatter. Two carried rifles.

"Go to hell, Charlie. What do you want me for?"

"You killed the Kid, Black Hawk and Henny they say— that leaves me, don't it?"

"You're doing the talking. Which one of you shot that boy?" He pressed himself to the side of the cabin to make less of a target, and wondered where the riflemen were at now. Then he saw one of them making a break across for some cover and snapped off a shot at him. The shooter went down screaming and holding his leg. That made five of them left.

"Tell your guys it won't come easy, Bowdry—that's two."

"You sumbitch, I'll get you. I knew you were at the races. Can't figure out why you ran out on me."

Good. Bowdry didn't know about the Abbott brothers being at Barren Forks. All right, for the next three hours he had to hold them off and then it would be dark. He reloaded his Colt while he had the chance, punching out and replacing the two cartridges. Then a rifle slug slapped the cabin side, and bits of dry bark stung his face. Instinctively he ducked. Time to get inside. The lack of windows in the cabin wouldn't help him, but the logs would absorb lots of lead. Two more slugs struck the wall as he dodged inside.

He crossed the room, and from the side of the back door he spotted two of them who must have thought he was still outside. One of them was waving for other to join him. Slocum took aim and dropped the waver in his tracks, then took a second shot at the other, who by then was fleeing. When the .44 slug hit him in the center of the back, the outlaw stiffened, then tripped and fell face-forward. That evened the odds a lot.

Slocum raced out the back door, covering lots of ground, and dove in the grass beside the first wounded man. He came up on his knees with the .44/40 Winchester that the outlaw had carried—jacked in a shell, took aim, and his first bullet struck the Morgan Bowdry sat on. Shot too low, damn. The hard-hit horse reared and then fell over sideways. Slocum winced over his mistake and cussed to himself.

Bowdry's cursing grew louder. "Bring me a damn horse!" But he never showed himself above the waist-high grass where he and his mount had gone down. There were three of them left. The other two, Slocum supposed, were on the far side of the cabin, and he wondered if they were tough enough to stand all this shooting. Not many men were ready to die, and unless they were desperate, the better part of valor for them would be getting the hell out while they were still unscathed.

He heard some horses running hard and hurried around the cabin to get sight of them. The two had gathered an extra horse and were riding low in the saddle, headed for the hatless Bowdry, who was running up hill to meet them. He made a flying mount, and they were gone from Slocum's rifle's range before he could even get one good shot off.

Maybe he'd made a believer out of them. He looked up and saw Bee by herself coming from the post oak thicket. She paused and looked at him, as if asking, was it all clear?

He nodded and went to the second prone outlaw. Bent

over, he rolled his limp body faceup and saw that the man's brown eyes were fixed on the sky. He found ten dollars in coins and cash on him, two knives, and undid the gunbelt, which he pulled off and slung over his shoulder.

"He got any money?" he asked her as she searched the still body of the rifleman.

"Few dollars—" She held a gold watch to her ear to listen and then shook her head. "It don't work."

"It's worth something," he said and eased off one of the man's dusty boots. Paper dollars flew like chicken feathers on the ground.

"Oh," she said, holding the "O" on her lips.

"Yes, they held up a train or two."

Before she reached for it, she paused and looked at him. "What we do with it?"

"Finders keepers."

She nodded and then pointed at her small breasts. "You and me split it?"

"Sure—fine. We better check that other guy's boots too." He heard something and swept up the rifle. In long strides he reached the side of the cabin to see the source. It was one of the wounded ones, and he was riding low in the saddle, making it hard for the ridge. That was all right; Slocum had no medical facilities for him anyway.

Long past sundown, the three dead men were lying in a common grave, and the fourth one was propped up to the side of the cabin barely hanging on. He'd been crushed under his horse's fall, and when Slocum returned from the grave, the man was coughing up blood. Slocum stopped and knelt on a knee.

"Was Two-hearts with you all?"

"Yeah . . . but . . . he got away."

"Who else besides Bowdry and him got away?"

"Billy Briggs . . . Wal . . . Walter Coffee."

"Where's Bowdry been staying?"

The man shook his head in the starlight to say that he

didn't know, and then he dropped his chin and Slocum knew he too was in the beyond.

She came to the door illuminated by the light from inside, and frowned. They exchanged looks and he nodded that the man was dead. Skirts in her hand, she came down the steps and took up his stocking feet. Then she looked at Slocum to say that she was ready to haul him away. "Room in that hole for one more, huh?"

"Yes, I made it wide." They carried the last one off to a common grave beyond the corral.

At the burial site, she stripped him down to his underwear like she had the others, to save the clothes, then rolled him in with them, which made a dull thud when he landed. Pushing off her knee, she rose. "I can cover them up in the morning. You come and eat now."

He yawned big and straightened. "I won't argue."

She hugged his waist and drove him toward the lighted door. "You make me plenty rich widow today."

He hugged her shoulder. "Sorry I made so damn much work out of it."

They both laughed going inside sideways.

The children were already asleep on pallets. He was picking his teeth after the meal as she washed her tin dishes on the dry sink in a chipped wash pan.

"I can buy some cows to run up here," she said, drying the last of them. "And a team and wagon."

"What happened to your man?"

"I heard he was killed."

"Heard?"

She nodded and then made a face like it didn't matter anymore. "He went to look for work one day and never came home. I wondered where he was, so I went up to Miami and asked around. Some guy up there said he had heard he was killed in a knife fight." She shook her head. "He didn't know where they buried him. So I came home."

"I see."

"I think we better celebrate all this money. I have no

whiskey, but . . ." She began to unbutton her dress in front of him and smiled at him. "I think we can do it in bed, huh?"

"I think so, little lady. I think so." And he toed off his boots,

Obviously she was anxious for him, for she blew out the candle, shed her dress and pulled him to the bed. In the darkness, he could only see the outlines of her small naked figure and outstretched arms. When he was between her knees on top, her small fingers began with earnest to pull on his increasing volume. When he was halfway hard, she raised her butt off the bed and started him into her tight pussy. His hips drove his spike into her, and she gasped, clutching him and pumping back to his every stroke. In a few minutes of fast action, she came. He eased back his thrusts until she recovered, and then again she grew fierce with him—and bang, she came again, and tossed her head as if lost. In a few minutes, he brought her back up to speed, and the ropes creaked under their hard action. He pumped in and out of her spasmodic contractions until he felt the hard cramp on his left nut and knew the end was coming. He grasped both sides of her tight ass and drove it home.

She gave a stifled cry and then wilted.

As they lay side by side in the bed, she stroked the beard stubble on his cheek. "I'm sure glad you came today. I sure needed this and that money too." Then she laughed. "They ever ask me, I can tell them you have big dick too."

He nodded and played with her small, hard breasts. "And I can say you are the woman who comes a lot."

"I never did that before today—never—wow."

"You sleepy?"

"No, you horny?"

"I could be."

She scooted closer and hugged him. "Then let's do it more."

Dawn came like a gray flannel sheet over the bluestem hills. He caught the two extra horses that came up to where his bay was in the corral and turned them inside after unsaddling them. He went to recover the two saddles off the dead horses—Bee would have a saddle shop when this was over. Bowdry's rig on the dead Morgan horse was hard to get undone, and he thought he'd need to pull it out with his horse. On his butt, he used his feet against the stiff corpse and at last jerked it free.

She had breakfast ready when the sun's spears began to shine around the hill.

"What will I do with all of their saddles and guns?"

"Trade 'em for cows." Seated at her table, he blew the steam off his coffee cup. "The rigs ought to bring four cows apiece."

She shook her head, acting impressed. "I don't know. They may call me Many-cows I do all that."

"It would be fine."

Embarrassed, she wet her lips, standing with the coffeepot ready for his refill. "You come this way again, you better stop."

"And see Many-cows?"

Her head bobbed and a straight smile filled her copper lips. "She will be here, and my children will have greasy mouths."

"How's that?"

"Now I can afford some pork. No more possum stew all the time."

She told him she would cover the bodies up and for him to go. Those men would not hurt her, but he should go in case they did come back. Then, with some tears in her lashes, she ran over and hugged him.

"May your medicine always be strong." Then with her face buried in his vest she said in low voice so her children could not hear, "Go now or I will have to take you to bed again."

20

He decided to drop by Hurricane's place one last time before he headed west to Council Oaks. In late afternoon, he dropped out of the timber and sat on his bay at the far end of the meadow. In the sun's bloody last minutes, nothing looked out of place as he studied the homestead. Hurricane's wagon was parked there in the yard. His team and saddle mule, grazing across the way, lifted their heads and looked in Slocum's direction. Something was amiss, and at first he couldn't be certain about the suspicions that made his stomach knot—then he realized that there was no smoke.

If they were at home, Blue would have a cooking fire going this time of day. He turned the bay back into the timber and circled around. Daylight was fast fleeting, and the shadows grew long faster and faster. Dry leaves rattled in the trees, and he kept an ear out for any sound—nothing. No strange horses in sight. None around the sheds or barn—he slipped off the bay in the cover of some head-high hickory sprouts and hitched him. Six-gun in his fist, he advanced on the main cabin as the sun slipped behind the horizon.

He reached the side of the building. His heart beat so loud it deafened him when he slipped in the back door. There had been a fight in there. Tables and chairs were overturned in the shadowy room, and the copper smell of blood filled his nose. In the growing darkness, he could see that Hurricane was tied in a high-back wooden chair, his head slumped forward. Not moving.

Satisfied he was alone, Slocum put up his Colt, struck a match and lit a candle on the table. He felt for a pulse behind Hurricane's ear. There was none. Damn, bound to a chair and then killed. Stabbed to death by some butcher that tortured him with his knife, one jab at a time.

"Oh, God, I'm sorry. I'm sorry I let this happen to you. You didn't deserve this." Tears flooded his eyes when he turned and discovered a worse sight on the bed. Blue's wrists were tied to the iron poster on each side above her—naked—bloody—the killer had carved her up like a madman, no doubt after they'd raped her. The gore—scalping her crotch even, probably before she died. What no-account dog would do such a thing?

Where was Wink? Her roan horse wasn't around—had they missed her? He decided to check the smaller cabin where they had held their lovemaking. He pulled the latchstring, shoved in the door, held the candle lamp up and the hinges creaked—nothing. For a long moment, he studied the faded quilt on the bed, simply relieved she wasn't in there. But if they got Hurricane and Blue, they sure wanted her too.

He needed to bury them—maybe Dora and Charlie would know something. Damn, he dreaded the job at hand. Heartsick, he turned an ear to the sounds of a horse coming. Were the killers coming back? His hand went to the grip of his .44—they better be wearing their go-to-hell clothes, 'cause they were going to get a bellyful of lead.

"Slocum!" Wink bolted off her horse and flew to him. "I thought you—"

"I wanted to check by—"

"What's wrong?"

Without words, he looked off in the darkness to find his lost speech, and set down his lamp. "There's been more bad things happen." He caught her by the waist. "You can't go in there. It's too bad."

She struggled to free herself by prying his hands away.

"Wink, damnit, take my word, it's the worst thing I've ever seen."

She straightened herself and swept the curls back from her face. "You said I had to be tough. I'm tough."

"Not enough for what's in there."

Her face set in the starlight, she reached for the candle lamp. He let go and followed her. It wasn't the way he wanted it.

Inside, she held the light up to shed it on Hurricane and gasped. "Savages," escaped her lips. Then she turned to the gruesome sight of Blue on the bed. Her hand flew to her mouth and she handed him the lamp, pushing past him with her hand extended straight out. On the porch's edge she vomited, then again and strangled.

"Who did this?" she managed to gasp when he joined her.

"I'm going to start with Two-hearts and go all the way to Bowdry."

"What must we do?"

"Dig two graves, and then we can ride to Barren Fork and settle with Two-hearts."

She closed her eyes and nodded in agreement. "Let's get started."

"How did you—"

"I went to Fort Smith to get my money out of the bank."

"You were going back to Kansas?"

She shook her head, not looking at him.

"None of my business—" He looked at her.

"I was going to hire a new man to kill Bowdry."

"You still can."

"I thought you were gone. Hurricane promised to find me someone."

"I guess he did," Slocum said and went for a pick and shovel. The gravelly hill ground would be tough to dig a

grave in, let alone two. She trailed after him, and they decided on a high place. At first it went easy, but soon he was
down to picking the clay loose each inch. By the time dawn
came, they were close to six foot deep and had decided to
widen as they went down to accommodate the two of them.

"They belong together," she said and he agreed.

The bodies wrapped in blankets, they placed them in the
grave and Slocum read the Twenty-third Psalm. Then they
went to covering them up. He hoped no evil spirits had gotten to his friends while he wasn't looking—Hurricane's people would have had a long wake guarding the bodies, firing
guns to ward off the evil ones, and his clansmen at the funeral would have made certain that no bad ones got in before
the bodies were delivered and covered.

Charlie and Dora came after they finished.

"What happened?" Charlie asked with a frown at the
fresh dirt.

Slocum told them the story. The two shook their heads
and Dora cried.

"Does he have any heirs?" Slocum asked.

"Maybe—" Charlie shook his head.

"You are the executor. I will write a paper and Wink will
witness it that he wanted you to take care of it," Slocum said.

"I can do that."

Slocum clapped him on the shoulder. "Thanks. We need
to ride."

"But you've been up all night—"

"We can sleep later. I'll see you again sometime." Slocum
went after the bay.

When he returned, Wink was on the roan. He took a paper
from his things and scribbled a note in pencil on the seat of
his saddle to the effect that Charlie was to be Hurricane's estate administrator. He had her sign it as witness. "This
should do."

He handed it to Charlie, shook his hand, mounted the
bay, and they were headed for Barren Fork. He waved to the
older pair and they left.

"Where will we go?" she asked as they trotted their horses down the dusty road littered with early fallen leaves.

"John Carter's. He's the one I know over there. Did he ever get his wife back?"

She smiled and shook her head, mildly amused. "Yes, but I'm not sure that she stayed."

Two days later they rode up to Carter's. Trail-weary and dust-floured, Slocum had looked over the place before they left the trees and came on up the road to the homestead. The beat of a hammer striking steel on an anvil made him feel secure, though he twisted several times in the saddle to look beyond the open fields for any sign of opposition.

"Hey Slocum, you're back," the sweaty-faced Cherokee said, looking up from his work on a horseshoe. He nodded to Wink and then mopped his face.

"I've got some bad news," Slocum said and dismounted. "Three days ago they murdered Hurricane and Blue."

"Oh, no."

"It was bloody. They must have tortured him for some time and—" He closed his lips tight and shook his head. "They did a tougher job on her, and probably made him watch them."

"Who?"

"I suspect Two-hearts. I had a run-in with Bowdry and his bunch up in the bluestem country. Didn't get him, but I got some of his gang. They must have swung back by and taken it out on Hurricane and Blue."

"I guess we can get the truth out of him." Carter began to shed his gloves and leather apron.

"We're ready now," Slocum said.

Carter looked pained at them. "You two look like some coffee and food might help."

"Don't go to any trouble—"

"No trouble, I'm batching again." He laughed and led them to the cabin.

Slocum glanced back and read the look on Wink's face—
I told you so.

After some leftover fried corn mush and coffee, they watered their horses while Carter saddled his.

"You have any plans?" she asked.

"Kind of play it by ear."

She nodded as if satisfied. "This is a tough business. I'm glad that you had me get in condition."

He gave her a confident nod. "You're doing well."

An hour later they were in the woods above Two-hearts's place. Smoke came from the chimney; Slocum was satisfied that someone was there. He shared a nod with Carter.

"We can get Hembree away from the house. We can squeeze the answers out of him," the tall Cherokee said.

"Slip down to the barn?" Slocum asked.

Carter agreed and they set out with her trailing them. They reached the barn, and Slocum could hear talking as they held tight to the board-and-bat siding.

". . . not be back till dark."

"Get away from me. Two-hearts will skin us both."

"He won't ever know we done it."

"I don't know . . ."

"Please?"

"All right, but make it quick."

Slocum nodded for Carter to go ahead, and they eased along the wall as the grunting began. He looked back to her, and she shook her head in disapproval. Carter drew his six-gun and Slocum followed. They stepped in the barn door.

In the shadowy light, Slocum could see that a bare ass was pumping between two brown legs, with her dress all wadded up under him. Holstering their guns, they ran over. Slocum jerked the man back. Carter smothered the woman's scream as she kicked and fought to get her dress down.

"Who're you?" Hembree blinked in shocked disbelief.

"Where did Two-hearts put the scalp?"

"What—what scalp?"

"The one he brought back with him a couple days ago." Slocum tightened his grip on the man's arm.

"I—I don't know."

"You better get to talking."

"Can I pull my pants up?" The man was trembling.

"I want an answer."

"It's—it's in the house on the wall."

Slocum let go, and the man quickly drew up his pants.

"What are you going to do to us?" the short, thin girl asked, looking at them visibly shaken.

"We're going to tell Two-hearts how you cheated on him," Slocum said.

"Oh, no!" she wailed. "He'll kill us."

"When's he coming back?"

She shrugged and shook his head. "He went for some whiskey."

Slocum and Carter nodded their heads—he'd be returning. "What's your name?"

"Wilma Nowater."

"He tell you that he'd killed Hurricane and his woman?"

Hembree looked off like he wasn't going to answer. Slocum reached out and shook his arm. "Answer me."

"I didn't want to hear it. I knew Hurricane; once he saved my mother from dying. Made me sick to hear his story of how he killed them."

"He say why?"

"He was mad. You killed his brother and he wanted revenge."

"Where's Bowdry?"

Hembree turned his palms up. "He doesn't stay here."

"Where does he stay?"

"Mrs. Fox's?" Carter asked.

"I think so," Hembree mumbled.

"Good. You know where she lives?" Slocum asked Carter.

"Down in the Arkansas River Valley."

Slocum shared a positive nod with Wink, who had stood back the whole time. "We're close. Damn close. Let's take them to the house and keep a fire going. I don't want him to think anything is changed. Two-hearts is no fool."

The two prisoners sat on chairs in the cabin with their hands tied. Carter had warned them if they yelled out any warning they'd be the first shot. Slocum split a lot of cooking wood and brought in two armsful. Wink brewed fresh coffee and rustled up some eggs and ham and made biscuits. The three enjoyed the meal and ignored their silent prisoners.

"Take a nap," Slocum said to her after the meal. "We'll wake you up when he comes. It could be hours."

Carter nodded in approval, cradling in his arms a rifle taken from the outlaw's things. "He may be drunk too when he comes back."

"Good," she agreed and stretched out on top of the quilts covering the bed. In minutes she was asleep.

Slocum held a cup of steaming coffee in his hands and considered the obscene scalp nailed on the cabin's wall. In his mind, he turned over and over the crime scene—it had been revenge against him for killing Two-hearts's brother. He shuddered under his shirt, despite the warm room. He'd be glad to have this over. *The sumbitch.*

"Someone is coming," Carter hissed.

"Think it is them?" Slocum hurried across the room. He stayed beside the door facing to be less conspicuous and tried to see the approaching horses.

"No, must be the law. They are all dressed up."

"Martin and Gaines are here," Slocum said to Wink as he woke her.

"Huh?"

"The U.S. marshals."

"What will we do?" she whispered.

"They want Two-hearts too."

"Hello the house."

"Hello," Slocum said and strode out. "Put your horses out of sight in the barn. We're expecting company."

Hap Gaines looked hard at him out of his right eye. "You're that White fellow we met a week or so ago. Lost his horses."

"Yeah, I figure you're looking for Two-hearts."

"Yes, we are. Wanted to ask him about a train robbery."

"Well, how about a double murder too? Put your horses up, we can talk and keep an eye out for him."

"He called you White?" Carter asked under his breath when the two led their horses to the barn.

"She's my missus too." He indicated Wink.

"Fine with me."

"Good, we can let the law handle him."

Past sundown, the loud singing of a drunk shattered the night. The four men nodded at one another. Hap and Slocum went out the back door, and once out the back, one went left and the other to the right to help cover the approaching outlaw.

"Hembree? Where in the fuck are you?" Two-hearts shouted.

"Right here," Hap said, advancing on the outlaw in the light coming from the front door. "Get them hands high or die."

"Where in the hell—"

In minutes, the killer stood in chains. Martin and Gaines both smiling, they drove him inside and forced him to sit on the floor.

Slocum untied Hembree and the girl. They both looked in fear at their former boss as they rubbed their wrists.

Hap Gaines interrogated Two-hearts, who said little more than grunts in reply. Martin took down the scalp as evidence and wrote a statement about it for her and Slocum to sign.

"Where's Booky James?" Gaines asked Hembree.

"Miami—"

"You dumb son of a bitch—don't tell them nothing. I get out of this, I'll nail your nuts to a stump."

Hembree fell backward as if to escape Two-hearts's wrath. Crashing into the table, he managed to get his footing and backed up to the far wall.

"He's small fish," Gaines said, to dismiss the matter. "Where's Bowdry?"

Obviously shaken by Two-hearts's threat, Hembree stood back, kept his lips sealed and shook his head.

"We're going to get some sleep," Slocum said, and the two excused themselves. They gathered their horses from the hillside woods, fed them corn from the crib and watered them. Then without a word to the lawmen they led their horses a good distance from the buildings, mounted and rode off in the starlight.

"Where're we going?" she asked.

"Salisaw and find Mrs. Fox."

"You know her?"

"We've met."

Wink laughed. "You know lots of folks."

"Lots know me too." He looked back in the inky light—nothing in sight. He was relieved to be out of there; he had considered pounding Two-hearts to death with his bare fists before they finally left the cabin. Let Judge Parker do that on his gallows. He'd sure miss Hurricane.

21

Late afternoon the next day, riding up the lane between two large fields, they approached a big white house. The cotton fields were white, and several blacks looked up from their picking. A few wagons sat at the end of the row, and a scales man nodded standing beside one and took off his felt hat for them when they reined up.

"Good-looking crop," Slocum said to the man.

"Yeah, it'll make a half a bale to the acre."

Slocum nodded. "Mrs. Fox at the house?"

"No, she's done gone to Fort Smith on business for a few days."

"Her friend Mr. Bowdry isn't here either?"

"No, sir, he went with her. Anything I can do?"

"I had some business to do with both of them. Reckon you know what hotel they are staying in?"

"Oh, they staying at the Wallace House out in Free Ferry Road. Wallace's are some kin of her late husband."

"Oh, yes," Slocum said as if he had forgotten. "What is Wallace's first name?"

"Gordon Wallace."

"Yes."

"You can't miss his place just past the Creekmore Bridge on the hill."

"Thanks. Guess we'll have to see them another time." He turned to her and she nodded in approval.

"Who shall I say has called?"

"Tom and Mrs. White."

"Yes, sir, I believe I've heard her talk about both of you."

"Fine lady. Give her our regards." He saluted him and they turned their horses back.

When they were out of his earshot, Wink leaned over and laughed softly. "Tom White, you're getting famous."

"He was just buttering up to me."

"I know. But is it safe for you to ride into Fort Smith?"

"If we want Bowdry, it is."

"All right, but I'll be worried."

"We ride hard enough, we can cross the ferry at sunrise and be at Alverson's place before anyone sees us."

"Means ride all night?"

"If we're going to get there."

"Who's Alverson?"

"A guy who owes me a favor."

She looked at the darkening sky for help. "Lots of folks owe you favors."

"Yes, ma'am, lots do, and I collect every chance I get. Let's ride." He pushed the bay into a trot.

Dawn was only on the napping ferry operator's imagination when in the starlight they descended the sandy bank laid in ties so the departing wagons did not sink. The man sat up, yawned big at their arrival and asked for forty cents. When they paid him and led their mounts aboard, he stoked up his steam engine, grumbling to himself about late night business until his stern-wheeler was frothing water and headed for the almost dark city on the far side.

On the far side they rode their horses up the vacant Garrison Avenue and soon were though the quiet business district of two- and three-story brick buildings, past the large

Catholic church, then down an alley that sent a few cats scurrying for cover. Slocum dismounted at a buggy house and slid the great door sideways. Several carriage and saddle horses nickered to him from their stalls. Wink led their horses inside and he stripped off the saddles.

"Who in the hell's in me stables?"

"No one, O'Riley."

"Well, saints pressure us, it's you down there, Slocum?"

"Yes and a lady too, so watch your language."

"I be biting me tongue. What brings you here?" He bowed to her in the light of the lamp he carried.

"A killer—we haven't slept in two days—"

"Well, pack yourself upstairs and both of you climb in me bed. I got to be up anyway. The boss he's going to Van Buren for a trial and needs the horse hitched and ready. I'll tell him not to disturb ya till he gets back—how's that?"

"Wonderful," Wink said and hugged the shorter man, who beamed after her small kiss to his face.

"I won't be washing it for a month," he said, patting his cheek.

"Tell your boss we'll see him this afternoon," Slocum said, leading her by the hand to the staircase.

"I sure will. But he'll be busting his buttons to know why you came."

"I'll explain it all tonight."

"Sleep well, me lady, and ya too, ya old devil." O'Riley laughed and bowed their departure.

Slocum found that small apartment reeked of pipe smoke. Needing no help, they pulled off their boots, lay across the bed in each other's arms and slept. Late afternoon the sounds of the doors rolling open and the arrival of a horse and buggy downstairs forced Slocum to sit up and stretch. He yawned big and reached over to shake her.

"Time to arise. Our host is back."

She said up and pushed the curls back from her face. "I must look a fright."

"You look fine, but you can freshen up; I'll go and talk to him."

"His name again?"

"Walter Alverson."

She nodded. "I'll do what I can."

Slocum pulled on his run-over dusty boots, tucked in his shirt and combed his hair with his fingers, then put on his hat and went down the steep stairs.

"My heaven, Slocum, what brings you here?" The tall man with gray sideburns, dressed in a well-tailored suit, met him and shook his hand.

"Needed a place to sleep mostly."

"Good heaven, why didn't you come in the house?"

"O'Riley was good enough to loan us his bed. I'm going to be leaving in a few hours and we won't impose on you very long."

"Nonsense, I haven't seen you in over a year. What have you been doing?"

"I'm after a killer that's here in Fort Smith. She's—" He tossed his head at the ceiling. "She's coming down. He shot her husband and son in a robbery in Kansas."

"My lands, who is he?"

"Charles Bowdry."

"And he's hiding here in town?"

"Out on Free Ferry Road at the Wallaces'."

"My heavens, Slocum, they are respectable people. Why hide a killer?"

"They don't know who he is."

"Oh, I see. What do you plan to do?"

"Go out there and take him in or kill him."

Alverson nodded as if in deep thought. "And the lady?"

"She wants to be there. He shot her son for no reason, and Bowdry along with his gang murdered Hurricane and his woman."

"The Cherokee medicine man?"

"Yes."

"When she comes down, both of you come to the

house—we'll have supper and I'll go out there with you. I know the Wallaces well."

"We're coming."

Alverson beamed. "My God, man, it's good to see you."

Slocum agreed with a bob of his head. "Same here."

Wink came down and fussed about him agreeing to go up to the house. "I'm sure not dressed for this. We've been in these clothes for a week."

"One more night won't hurt us," he said and told O'Riley he'd see him later.

"Ya's be wanting them ponies saddled?"

"Yes, thanks."

"Thank you a lot. I loved your bed," she said and laughed.

"Aw, it's me pleasure, dear lady. Glad you could sleep. They'll be ready when you come back," he said after them.

Alverson's gray-headed housekeeper scurried about setting the table and introduced herself to Wink while the men went off to sip good whiskey in the drawing room.

"Is this the Captain Bowdry I know about from the army days?" Alverson asked.

"Yes, since the war got over, he made himself colonel. Your law firm must be doing well."

"Doing well. This area is booming. Railroads pushing in from the east and north. Fort Smith may soon become the center of the nation. Wallaces?"

"Mrs. Fox's husband's relatives, I understand. He's been staying with her."

"Charming lady. Cherokee, isn't she?"

"Yes. Her late husband left her rich enough."

"Oh, his estate is unimaginably large. What in the hell does she see in Bowdry?"

"I think she likes to live on the edge."

"Interesting. Tell me about the lady with you."

Slocum told him some of the details about her before Renna called them to supper. Alverson put on his charm for Wink and acted like she was a well-dressed woman at a fancy restaurant. The fried chicken, flour gravy, green beans and mashed potatoes all tasted fresh. A magnificent meal topped off with Renna's pecan pie.

Alverson and Wink's conversation went on and on, until they both blinked as if discovering Slocum was there when he said, "Time to go."

The three rode their saddle horses down the bloody alleyway as the sun dropped into the Indian Nation. Twilight had begun to set in when they crossed the Creekmore Bridge and climbed the hill. Alverson nodded to a two-story brick mansion and they reined down the driveway.

Riding three abreast down the lane between rail fences, Wink shook her head as if saddened.

"What's wrong?" Slocum asked her.

"This was how they rode up to the store that day. I was on the porch dumping my mop bucket and watched them."

He nodded that he'd heard her, seeing lights coming on in the house. "You two watch out. There may be shooting when he sees me."

"We'll be careful," Alverson said.

They drew up at the front stairs. A black houseman came out to the edge. "Gentlemen," he bowed to her, "Ma'am, may I's help you?"

"Yes, I wish to speak to Colonel Bowdry."

"I am afraid there be no one here by that name, sah."

"Tell Mrs. Fox's man to come out here," Slocum said, feeling a chill go up his jaw bone.

"But, sah—"

"I said. Tell him to get out here now."

"Yes, sah."

"NO!" a woman screamed and rushed out on the porch. Slocum heard a door slam and put heels to the bay. Bowdry was going out the back way. Slocum drove the horse around the house in time to see a white shirt as Bowdry jumped the rail fence.

"Hold it, Bowdry." He reined up the horse. No response, he fired low and the outlaw went down. Slocum bailed off the bay and landed on the ground across the fence.

On the run after him, he saw the muzzle flash. Bowdry had fired a shot at him. Slocum paused and aimed at the white shirt that looked stark in the starlight centered in on the dark meadow. He returned fire, cocking the pistol each time and counting—last one was for her son, one for her husband, one for Hurricane and one for Blue.

"No, no," Mrs. Fox cried. Holding her skirts, she raced past him to the fallen killer.

Slocum reloaded his Colt, then started that way.

"How could you?" she screamed at him, hugging the bloody Bowdry and rocking him in her lap. "He's dying."

"It just ain't fast enough for all he's done bad," he said to her and turned, holstered his gun. "It's over," he said to Wink, stopping her from going back there. "Let her be alone."

"They sent for the law," Alverson said.

"You can explain it. And take care of her for me." He motioned to Wink.

"Of course, my pleasure. And you?"

"I've got places to be." He took Wink by the arms and kissed her hard.

"I owe you—" she pleaded.

Slocum shook his head at her and started for his horse. Filled with enough hurt to cut off his breath, he mounted the bay, took the free ferry to Van Buren and never looked back till he rode up the Log Cabin Hill Road to the top of the bluffs. From there he could see the Arkansas River as it snaked around the flickering lights of Fort Smith.

Somewhere he needed to send a telegram to Santa Fe to tell a man she was free—maybe, if Alverson let her get away. He looked at the old North Star—since he was headed northwest anyway, he might go by and check on Bee *Manycows* and see how she was making it—might need some branding done. Weather held, he could still be in San Antonio before it got too cold.

He booted the bay on.

Watch for

SLOCUM AT DEAD DOG

338th novel in the exciting SLOCUM series
from Jove

Coming in April!

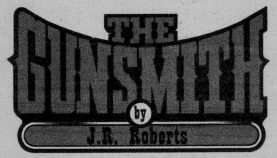